More Critical Praise for Achy C

for *Days of Awe*

"Obejas masterfully links identity with place, language, and the erotic life, without ever descending into sentimentality . . . Her descriptions render her characters' emotional lives with a precision that precludes exotic stereotyping. [A] focus on language accounts for one of the novel's most enchanting riches, revealing a capacity to neatly articulate in Spanish the concepts that English and other languages have no words for."

—*Los Angeles Times*

"Obejas relates the compelling and disquieting history of Judaism and anti-Semitism in Cuba amidst evocative musings on exile, oppression, inheritance, the unexpected consequences of actions both weak and heroic, and the unruliness of desire and love . . . Richly imagined and deeply humanitarian, Obejas's arresting second novel keenly dramatizes the anguish of concealed identities, severed ties, and sorely tested faiths, be they religious, political, or romantic."

—*Booklist* (starred review)

"An ambitious work . . . A deft talent whose approach to sex, religion, and ethnicity is keenly provocative."

—*Miami Herald*

"With intelligent, intense writing, Obejas approaches, in ambition, the heady climes of Cuban American stalwarts Oscar Hijuelos and Cristina Garcia. Highly recommended . . ."

—*Library Journal*

"[A] clear-eyed, remarkably fresh meditation on familiar but perennially vital themes."

—*Publishers Weekly*

"[A] soulful, erotically charged, and densely woven meditation on public and private identity . . . *Days of Awe* is an impressive, almost magical-realistic exploration of Cuban culture, the meaning of exile, and the many roles the closet plays in the history of human identity . . . Obejas's deft historical eye for the infinitely subtle gray scale of race, religion, and sexuality is a triumph."

—*The Advocate*

"Obejas writes a rich and sonorous prose and tells her tale obliquely, with shifts and leaps in time and space . . . She shows that ideas and inspiration are close at hand in a time of cross-cultural ferment, when the world is shrinking and empires are crumbling. There's plenty of reason to hope for the future of a fiction that welcomes writers with such a passionate sense of the past, both personal and cultural."

—*San Jose Mercury News*

"Achy Obejas has woven together an intricate story of cultural and ethnic intermingling that greatly enriches our understanding of our world and ourselves. Her prose is rich and poetic, and her characters are appealing in their very ambiguity."

—*Americas*

"Achy Obejas in wise fashion tackles touchy issues in the Cuban exile—to be a Jew in the closet, to be gay, always going upstream but always yearning for the homeland. She takes on issues of the Cuban community that have been overshadowed by the never-ending political debate around the future of Cuba after Fidel Castro."

—*Chicago Sun-Times*

for *Memory Mambo*

"The power and meaning of memory lie at the heart of Obejas's insightful and excellent second work of fiction. With prose so crisp, the book could pass for a biography . . . This is an evocative work that illuminates the delicate complexities of self-deception and self-respect, and the importance of love and family."

—*Publishers Weekly*

"Adept at stream-of-consciousness narrative, Obejas fulfills the musical promise of her title, and mambos her way through this seamless, seductive, and, ultimately, disturbing tale about a time of crisis in the life of a young Latina . . . Raw, powerful, and uncompromising."

—*Booklist*

"Nothing in Obejas's story is romanticized. Her work is about exposing truth . . . She writes a graphically poignant story about believable and interesting characters drawn from experiences close to home.

—*Washington Post*

"*Memory Mambo* insists on the truth, which in the hands of Achy Obejas is dark, witty, and haunting in its complexity. Achy Obejas is a supremely talented story-teller with a gift for dialogue, character development, and insight into the human condition. *Memory Mambo* is a memorable novel from the first page to the last."

—*Midwest Book Review*

"Its complex story folds back on itself constantly, moving fluidly through time, and through the memories and histories of its many characters."

—*Village Voice*

"The melancholy and sense of displacement that is in the background of Obejas's collection of humorous short stories is at the heart of *Memory Mambo,* her first novel . . . Her characters are as flawed and as worthy of compassion as we are; whether we identify as Latino/a, gay, and working class, we are all of us *primos* of exile. Recommended."

—*Library Journal*

Ruins

Achy Obejas

AKASHIC BOOKS
NEW YORK

This is a work of fiction. All names, characters, places, and incidents are the product of the author's imagination. Any resemblance to real events or persons, living or dead, is entirely coincidental.

Grateful acknowledgment is made to the estate of Nicolás Guillén for permission to reprint "Tengo" (1964) on pages 91–93; translation by Achy Obejas. The italicized passage at the top of page 181 is a quote from "La Isla en Peso" by Virgilio Piñera (1943); translation by Achy Obejas.

Published by Akashic Books
©2009 Achy Obejas

ISBN-13: 978-1-933354-69-9
Library of Congress Control Number: 2008925940
All rights reserved

First printing

Akashic Books
PO Box 1456
New York, NY 10009
info@akashicbooks.com
www.akashicbooks.com

Para Cary, Eliana, Oscar Luis, Barbarita,
y todos mis vecinos en Tejadillo,

y para Miguel

Acknowledgments

Thanks to Rafael Acosta, Alejandro Aguilar, Violeta Alvárez, Megan Bayles, Patrick Bergman, Florentina Boti, Christina Brown, Kalisha Buckhanon, Cintas Foundation, Jimena Codina, Norberto Codina, Natasha Díaz Argüelles, David Driscoll, Catherine Edelman, Argelia Fernández, Ambrosio Fornet, Sarah Frank, Carlos Garaicoa (for the giants), Gisela González López, Manuel González, Anna Hirsch, Elise Johnson, Meredith Kaffel, Janice Knight, Llilian Llanes, Carolyn Kim, Leona Nevler, Jim O'Shea, Bajo Ojikutu, Patricia Peláez, Esther Pérez, Don Rattner, Patrick Reichard, Lucía Sardiñas, Charlotte Sheedy, Alma Sías, and María de los Ángeles Torres.

At the *Chicago Tribune*, I'm especially grateful to Geoff Brown, Peter Kendall, Nannette Smith, Kaarin Tisue, James Warren, and everybody in research, especially David Turim.

At the Pilchuck School of Glass, I was ably taught in so many ways by so many: Rik Allen, Marielle Brinkman, Lucinda Doran, Barbara Johns, Paul Larned, Jeremy Lepisto, Steve Marino, Dimitri Michaelides, Pike Powers, and Chuck Vannatta.

At DePaul University, I live in awe of my colleagues in Latin American and Latino Studies: Sylvia Escárcega, Camila Fojas, John Tofik Karam, Felix Másud-Piloto, Lourdes Torres, and the two most efficient women who've ever run an office, Cristina Ródriguez and María Ochoa.

I'm in debt to my friend, the writer Arturo Arango, longtime Cojímar resident and witness to the exodus of 1994, who shared his memories of the time with me in correspondence and conversation.

The first chapter of this novel appeared, in slightly different form, in the *Indiana Review,* Vol. 25, No. 1, and I thank the editors for their early and fervent belief in the story.

Thanks, too, to Johnny Temple and the good, good folks at Akashic.

Lastly, this book benefited from the patience, love, and power of two very special people: Tania Bruguera and Eva Wilhelm. Mil, mil gracias.

I am tired, I am weary
I could sleep for a thousand years
A thousand dreams that would awake me
Different colors made of tears
—The Velvet Underground, "Venus in Furs"

I.

U snavy was an old man. Not in age so much—he had turned fifty-four that year—but he was born old, his childhood brow prematurely molded into an expression of permanent concern, his gait, even as a youngster, as labored as if he'd been instantly injured on the job, both in spirit and in fact. His pale gray eyes sat in his mushroom-brown face, common and faded, even in boyhood, as if they'd never twinkled or delighted with wonder or awe.

All that summer of 1994, Usnavy had manned his post at the bodega—the one where people came with their ration books to have their monthly quotas of rice and beans and cooking oil doled out—and wordlessly shook his head when people pointed to a page for an item they should have received but which he didn't have to give. His eyes darted over the void on his side of the counter: soap was scarce, coffee rare; no one could remember the last time there was meat. Sometimes all he had was rice or, worse, those detestable peas used to supplement beans or, when ground up, used as a coffee substitute.

Now and then, when the shelves were particularly bare, he would find himself involuntarily thinking about Belgian chocolates, the kind his mother used to crave: in a box, each nugget tucked into a white paper nest. He imagined giving such a box to his wife, Lidia, and watching her and their fourteen-year-old daughter, Nena, laugh as they shared the sweets, their fingers dotted with cacao peaks. Nothing brought him greater joy than their pleasure; nothing affected him quite like his daughter walking beside him, her fingers laced with his.

At the bodega, Usnavy knew he shouldn't be partial with what was available. He needed to weigh it out and pour it into the bag for whomever got there first—but Usnavy tried to hoard the bulk of it, just in case, for the most needy: the solitary elderly and the young mothers with kids like kittens clawing at their hems, frantic and unaware that their fathers had hurled themselves into the sea on toothpicks, desperately trying to reach other shores for better luck. After a windsurfing instructor from Varadero had illegally managed the waves all the way to the Florida Keys in little more than nine hours, scores of young men were now seen erecting homemade sails on boards all over the coasts, feigning interest in things like barometric pressure and practicing their skills walking on water.

Usnavy stared at those leaving in disbelief. He wanted to tell them that fate was not in a shoreline or a flag, but in a person's character. Yet to confront the windsurfers and other mariners meant dealing with the fierceness of their desire—and even Usnavy understood that if the blinding light bouncing off the mirrored waves did not obscure their focus, there was nothing that would keep them from seeing what they wanted to see. They were, each and every one, like Christopher Columbus, insistent on a mainland filled with promise, no matter the truth of the island.

After the morning shift, when the sun was hottest and heaviest, Usnavy would shuffle back home to his family's Old Havana apartment on Tejadillo street, a windowless high-ceilinged room, no bigger than one of those bloated American cars. Concrete on all six sides, Usnavy's room in the tenement distorted daylight and time but remained relatively cool throughout the worst of days. A picture of a young Comandante hung in a frame, their only decoration but for a poster of the American singer Michael Jackson, which Nena had gotten as a gift from a friend down the street who'd left for the United States a few years before.

Besides the bed, there was a folded cot, where Usnavy slept so Lidia and Nena could be more comfortable, and a tiny table with a Czech-made electric plate he'd received from the Prague-born wife of a Cuban friend when they had hurried back to her country after the communists tumbled. Next to the plate was a small, white, Soviet refrigerator. Usually, Lidia's old American iron—much coveted, since irons of every lineage had virtually vanished in the last few years—rested on top, cushioned by a threadbare but very clean towel.

There were books all over the room too, on homemade shelves, tucked under Nena and Lidia's bed in neat rows, and usually in piles next to it as well. Not just Nena's school books but also books about Africa, poetry books, books with ambiguous endings by Jorge Luis Borges and Chester Himes (beautifully translated into Spanish), and a young Cuban writer named Leonardo Padura, one of Usnavy's recent favorites, whose work had been published in Spain and Mexico.

On the wall behind the door, there were a pair of hooks on which Usnavy hinged his bike, his only means of transportation and one of the few things over which he and Nena had occasional arguments. About this, Usnavy was intractable, refusing to surrender his one chance at relief and escape. His official excuse for refusing to let her borrow it was that he couldn't risk the bike being stolen from her. But in his thinking, she didn't need a bike: Her school was only a few blocks up, by the capitol building. Of course, Nena was a teenager now and naturally restless. She wanted to be out, to go, anywhere. In his heart Usnavy understood it would be better if she had her own bike, but he simply couldn't afford it. So as much as he hated to think about it, she'd have to continue walking to get around, hitchhiking like everyone else, and taking the bus, which he knew was often hours late, crowded, and a source of other kinds of dangers too.

Sometimes, he knew, the bus didn't show up at all. Since the scarcity of fuel had forced the government to cut public transportation service down to bare bones, Lidia, a hospital taxi driver for more than twenty years—one of the first women to really excel at the job—had been laid off and now just shuffled around Tejadillo in a faded housedress most of the time, stunned if not bitter, not because she'd lost her job but because younger men with much less experience had been allowed to stay on.

"They have family," Usnavy had tried to explain to her.

In the first few months of her layoff, the government had given Lidia a good chunk of her old salary in compensation, but after she'd taken a reeducation course in arts and crafts her take-home pay had been dramatically and embarrassingly reduced. Though she was licensed now as an artisan, there was no paper, no ink, no paint, nothing. The two or three practice prints she'd made in class of Che Guevara and views of dawn in the tropics were smears of color, indecipherable, and long since shredded for note taking and other more intimate uses.

Now, whenever Usnavy tried to rationalize things for her, Lidia bit her trembling lip and looked away, refusing to make eye contact with him, leaving him frazzled and frail.

To relieve the gloom, the family's room—a breadbox, a shoebox—was illuminated by a most extraordinary lamp. Were it not for the sheer size of it, Usnavy could have built a second floor—a barbacoa—like many of his neighbors. Made of multicolored stained glass and shaped like an oversized dome, the lamp was wild. Almost two meters across, the cupola dropped down with a mild green vine-and-leaf motif that flowered into luscious yellow and red blossoms, then became a crimson jungle with huge feline eyes. (In truth, they were peacock feathers, but Usnavy had never seen or dreamt of peacocks, so he imagined them as lions or, at least, cats.) The armature consisted of branches at the top, black and fat to resemble the density of tree bark. They narrowed as they neared the edge, until they were pencil thin and delicate. The borders were shaped with the unevenness of leaves and eyelids, petals and orbs, in a riotous yet precise design.

Because Usnavy lived in the old colonial district, in a tenement carved out of a nineteenth-century mansion with twisted and enigmatic electric wiring that refused to respond to a central command, while the rest of Havana—in fact, the rest of Cuba—suffered long, maddening power outages and blackouts, Usnavy and his family never lacked the glow of his majestic lamp.

The lamp had traveled with Usnavy from his hometown of Caimanera, the closest Cuban town to the American military base at Guantánamo Bay and the reason for his unusual name: Gazing out her window at the gigantic military installation, Usnavy's mother had spied the powerful U.S. ships, their sides emblazoned with the military trademark, which she then bestowed on her only son. She pronounced it according to Spanish grammar rules—*Uss-nah-veee*—and for a while caused something of a stir, which other young mothers soon imitated so that by the time the Revolution was upon them, there was a whole tribe of sturdy young Usnavys in Oriente. (In the 1980s, during the Soviet boom in Cuba, there was another inexplicable surge of English-inspired names, particularly Milaydy, Yusimí—*You-see-me*—and Norge, after the refrigerator company.) Usnavy—the original one: Usnavy Martín Leyva—was born in 1940, shortly before Pearl Harbor, when the U.S. might have been thrown off balance but instead sailed off to eager battle the way young people—ignorant of their mortality—recklessly throw themselves into love or revolution. Perhaps as a result of all that, Usnavy carried with him a kind of guilt: At one time, it was possible his mother had loved the enemy (in all fairness, they hadn't been seen or understood, exactly, as the enemy then), had aspired to the enemy's might, had tried to project onto him their sense of possibility and optimism.

His father—as Usnavy had been told, a Jamaican laborer (a poor schmuck, he had surmised)—had disappeared into the sea, leaving his mother a widow shortly after he was born, free to rearrange the past at will and dream about the future.

Usnavy remembered her in the radiance of that marvelous lamp—a rush of light in a splendid drawing room at a house called *The Brooklyn*, where important men sat for hours and chatted and smoked while swaying on colonial-style rocking chairs. They played cards and talked of vital things in many languages, like drilling for oil in Texas and African safaris. They bragged about their rhino noses, lion pelts, and elephant tusks, prizes taken from the Serengeti, the stolen home of the Maasai. All the while, a young Usnavy hovered about in the margins, dizzy from the cigar smoke and the buzzing voices. He imagined himself not a hunter or a stateless native, but one with the beautiful beasts, feral and unbound. As each tale of adventure unfolded under the glorious lamp, Usnavy would feel his heart racing, as if absorbing the shock of the shot, from the depth of his guts to the tangle and blockage in his throat. He'd cough and gag until it passed, his mother stroking his young, blondish locks in a contained panic. The men just drank their whiskey, passed bills among themselves, and signed papers.

Usnavy had a memory of his mother as a charming presence, young and tender in the glow. When she moved to Havana many years later, he was comforted to see the lamp in her possession. The luminescence kept her youthful somehow, so that Usnavy never had a memory of her as old, as if the crone whose features served as the only model for his own was a neighbor instead of his mother. She hovered in his peripheral vision, as tantalizingly close and out of reach as a promise. Her burial was a favor he executed for someone he was only remotely connected to, an act of charity meant to ameliorate her aloneness and prove that, in Cuba anyway, no one died without the benefit of community. At his mother's passing, the lamp was Usnavy's only inheritance, which he accepted like a reward for exemplary revolutionary work.

In the damp and acrid tenement, the lamp was a vibrant African moon in a room that was by nature s pectral. It was delicate and oversized in a place that demanded discretion and toughness—if it swayed, it might shatter against the concrete. But Usnavy insisted on displaying it.

"What good does it do packed away?" he'd asked Lidia (as if storing it somewhere else were an actual option). "Let's just enjoy it, it's so lovely."

Lately, he knew Lidia fretted because their upstairs neighbors—in violation of both the law and logic—had built up from their second floor room, adding another whole tier for themselves on the roof. Using bricks scavenged from the many edifices that had crumbled in recent times, the neighbors had nearly doubled their space, but the weight of the new construction was taking its toll. In Usnavy's room, the ceiling already had small cracks, and Lidia had spotted a line of water yellowing the plaster, circling the spot where the lamp was attached. She had tried talking to the neighbors but they dismissed her worries. And when she mentioned it to her husband, he just nodded, never quite register-ing her concern.

"I'll talk to them, I promise," he'd tell her, but he seemed to regard his lamp as invulnerable, and the talk with the neighbors kept dropping on his list of things to do until Lidia became resigned to the problem and the peril.

In the meantime, Usnavy's only preoccupation seemed to be, as always, maintaining the lamp's cleanliness and shine, polishing it as if it were a piece of treasure dug up from the sea.

Lidia would stare up at him, as if about to ask something: Her lips would part slightly, quiver, then close again.

Usnavy would stand barefoot on the bed where Lidia and Nena slept and reach up and rub each of the little glass panels with a silk cloth guaranteed not to streak or scratch. A couple of the panels had hairline fractures; Usnavy knew they could pop with the slightest push and he was especially gentle around them.

At night, he kept the light on until the last possible second, engaged in a never-ending staring contest with the lamp's feline eyes. Some-times, especially when she was younger, his daughter Nena would curl into the curve under his arm and join him, imagining all the possibili-ties within the lamp's vast offerings. That, she'd say, aiming a finger at a green slice of light, was the fertile Nile traversing the continent, and that, he'd point out in the opaqueness of a tiny triangle, the whirling sands on the beaches of Madagascar.

But these days Usnavy was on his own. Now Nena would bury her head under the sheet, ignoring Africa—ignoring him—and sigh loudly and repeatedly until Usnavy finally pulled the lamp's cord and darkness imploded.

* * *

Outside the door of their room in the tenement, Usnavy and his family had a big metal barrel of water which he guarded zealously with a lock and chain, and which they used by filling a plastic bottle or bucket and carrying that to the bathroom in the middle of the courtyard, a swirling funnel of flies shared with the rest of the tenants (now too numerous to count). The water was hard, almost metallic, swimming with so many invisible parasites that it was imperative not to swallow even when brushing one's teeth. Everything had to be boiled, the steam rising in the tropical heat like a malevolent and cruel ghost.

There was no light in the bathroom except what came in through a broken window where the local boys would lurk and peek, so that at night it was essential to carry the fortitude for argument and a torch made from rolled-up newspapers. (Flashlights and candles had long disappeared from Havana.) Sometimes in the dark, Usnavy would imagine breaking off a part of the lamp—a lump of fiery orange and red, one of those brilliant eyes—and using it to light his way instead.

What struck Usnavy most these days was how many strangers suddenly surrounded him. Not that long ago, he knew everyone who lived on Tejadillo. But in the last year, at least thirty people had left, mostly young men, a few young women—all of them by boat or balsa, wobbly and dangerous. Their rooms were instantly taken over by supposed relatives from the provinces—large, overflowing families, with dozens of kids and so many cousins. They sometimes brought roosters with them, small pigs, a goat once.

For Usnavy, the relatives were a blur, a vague echo of his original neighbors. He couldn't keep all their names straight. He could barely tell them apart. Worst of all, what had once seemed to him like a safe harbor, now struck him as alien and claustrophobic, a pirate's cove.

* * *

By early evening, when everyone in the tenement sat on the stoop playing Parcheesi and chess (using beans, shells, and pebbles for game pieces), or milled about the courtyard, Usnavy would wash up in the communal bathroom, and then ride his bike down to the docks, enjoying the moist breeze but also wistful about the now empty harbor: Gone were the Soviet vessels and those of their former friends from the socialist bloc. The Russians, with their cryptic lettering, would leave no sons named after powerful ships or armed forces in Cuba, only a pedestrian Pavel here and there and the predictable Ivans and Vladimirs.

Most nights after a meager dinner of rice—that's about all there was these days, occasionally accompanied by a dollop of beans or the fried remains of a grapefruit rind—Usnavy would seek relief in a game of dominos under the trees at a tiny park down narrow Montserrate, playing with a few other men his age who'd sit on boxes and strategize, slapping the thick pieces down with grunts and puffs of blue cigar smoke.

"Guapo!" a cocky-looking character called out when he saw Usnavy approaching. That could mean *Handsome* or *Gutsy* but it was hard to say what was intended in this case, since the fellow shouting was Frank, one of Usnavy's oldest friends, but a guy known as a wiseass, even a little cruel sometimes.

Usnavy's stomach made a screeching noise. He was late because he'd gone with Nena to get a copy of her birth certificate at the civil registry in Playa district, only to be told they only had documents through 1976—before Nena's 1980 birth—so she'd have to go back to the one in Old Havana.

Recently, Nena had lost her identification card, which had turned into a bureaucratic nightmare that now had him mortified and her seething. Discovering the initial loss, Nena had gone immediately to the Old Havana office that issued the ID cards all Cubans needed to carry with them. But there she was told they had no record at all of her, that her documents must be in Playa, where they had lived with Lidia's parents when Nena was born.

"But they're the ones who sent us here," Usnavy pleaded.

The clerk shrugged. "What do you want me to do?" he asked blandly.

Overhead a fan whipped the hot air about, the rusty blades squeaking as they turned. Nena sighed, wiping a line of moisture from her lip, waving her father away as he tried to explain that these things can happen anywhere in the world.

He hated that, these days, every little detail had other meanings. A casual stumble could be turned into an essay on ineptness—if not by Nena, then by any of her friends or schoolmates; nowadays, Usnavy thought, anyone at all could twist things around, make things look worse than they really were. He lived in fear of how that dynamic could affect Nena, how it could drive her someday to the shores, like all those crazy rafters and windsurfers, to look for relief on the horizon.

Days later, at the Old Havana office, when Nena's papers were pronounced missing one more time and another clerk instructed them to go back again to the civil registry in Playa to get a new birth certificate, Nena declared herself lost to society.

"If you want me to carry my own ID, Papi, then you get it," she said, not in a spoiled way, not out of defiance, but out of exasperation. This was exactly what Usnavy was afraid of, that frustration over something so minor would throw her off the righteous path. He glared at the clerk, wanting to kill the messenger right there and then.

"We have a copy of your birth certificate at home, under the bed,"

Usnavy told his daughter, not keen at all on her being lost to society. "Don't worry."

But when they got to Tejadillo, he discovered that their photostatic copy of her birth certificate had been ruined by dampness and age. A green circle of mildew pretended to officialize it with its own seal.

Nena sighed long and deep and shook her head before leaving the family's room to go hang out with her friends, which made Usnavy anxious. He knew he couldn't lock her up but how he wished he could; how he wished he could keep her from telling this story, in which so much lent itself to misreading and manipulation.

A few days later, though it had taken quite a bit of coaxing to get her to come along yet again to the Old Havana office, Usnavy tried to squelch his irritation and concern as they strolled together through the office doors. But when they entered this time—sweaty, covered with grime after the long bike ride with Nena balanced on the handlebars— they discovered it was being painted and they'd have to come back yet again in a few days. The office smelled fresh, implied a future.

The same clerk they'd seen before was busy pouring paint from one can into another. On the way out, he offered to sell some to Usnavy. It was an institutional ivory color, which Usnavy declined instinctively.

I will maintain my integrity, I will be free of reproach, he swore to himself. As he turned away from the temptation, he glimpsed Nena's expression—a mix of resignation and disbelief. It was true their room needed painting. But there was no way he was going to buy that paint illegally. They would do what they'd always done: wait their turn, wait until their request was formally and legally approved.

Nena sighed again—a long and quiet breath. This time Usnavy joined her, inadvertently catching himself exhaling as if coming out of some Zen exercise, trying to keep his mind clear.

* * *

The domino players on Montserrate were Usnavy's childhood pals, men who'd enjoyed and endured together. But Usnavy, though he knew he was appreciated as much as any of the others, also knew he stood apart from them. They were criollos—Cuban-born, all of them—and they were well aware that Usnavy had been birthed right there too, in Caimanera, amidst the bloody sheets that covered a bed at a rooming house called *Indiana* (before he and his mother moved up to *The Brooklyn*), but they insisted, now and again, on calling him El Yanqui, even though he'd explained over and over that his father was Jamaican, a worker at the U.S. base, who ate salt pork and spoke English with a lilt (though, truth be told, he had no memory of him at all, just his mother's brief stories, prompted only when a young Usnavy would ask).

But Frank and the other boys didn't care. They looked at Usnavy's fair skin and reddish-blond hair as a boy and laughed, called him Tom Sawyer, called him Mickey (after the American actor Mickey Rooney), but mostly El Yanqui, which irked Usnavy always, even long before the Revolution. That's about when they backed off, after years of taunting him with that, because they knew—they were friends, after all—that calling somebody El Yanqui might have other meaning or consequences then.

They had all celebrated the triumph of the Revolution together. They'd been warriors in the rebel army's largest battalion, the Sixth Column, composed entirely of boys from Oriente just like them: poor boys, orphaned boys, boys who—with the exception of Frank and, to a lesser extent, Diosdado—couldn't read or write much beyond their names; young men who waved the black-and-red 26th of July flag and saw Che as a kind of real-life Errol Flynn.

It was because of that fortuitous affiliation (a lark for most of them, actually) that they all wound up in Havana together, when the Sixth Column was turned into the capital's first revolutionary police force. Now products of the literacy campaign, the Sixth Column also founded the Revolution's first magazine, *Rebelde Seis*, but only Frank participated in that, and only Usnavy kept copies, right there under the bed next to the now classic—and somewhat problematic—back issues of *Lunes de Revolución* and a thin little volume of stories by Calvert Casey, published on faint, splotchy paper.

As the years passed, things changed for each of the friends, like for so many others: Frank—the smart one, he'd been educated before the Revolution in Quaker and Baptist schools in Holguín—found his opportunities limited and lost his badge because he refused to abandon his faith (although later he became an atheist on his own; a logical evolution, he claimed, resulting from experience). At one point, Obdulio's brother left the country by jumping the fence from Caimanera to the U.S. base, and then Obdulio began getting pressure from his sergeant to stop writing to his exiled kin. Years later, Diosdado's effeminate son, Reynaldo, was arrested because he wore lipstick in public or some such stupidity (as far as Usnavy was concerned, both the lipstick and the arrest were ranked at the same level of inanity), and that was that—everyone knew the boy would be on the first raft he could get on. Finally, Mayito—his wife and children in New York thanks to an American relative Mayito had never known she had—had resigned from the force, embarrassed by his wife's antirevolutionary stands, before he was isolated by his peers. After biding his time for years, expecting her to return admonished by the horrors of capitalism, now he waited instead for her claims to go through immigration and for his U.S. visa to arrive.

One by one, Usnavy's friends had begun to question, then doubt, then snicker, then openly joke about the situation, sometimes good-naturedly, often bitterly.

"It was good, it was right at the beginning," Obdulio would say, "but you have to admit, Usnavy, it didn't turn out exactly like we thought it would."

"All this sacrificing for tomorrow," Frank would chime in, "and tomorrow never comes."

"One hundred years from now, will anyone remember what we did here?" asked Obdulio, but it was a rhetorical question; he was shaking his head.

"And whatever goes wrong is always somebody's else's fault!" added Diosdado. "After thirty-five years, don't you think it's time somebody else got a chance to see what they can do? After thirty-five years, haven't we produced anybody who can step up?"

"What remains, huh?" asked Frank.

But Usnavy, the only one who'd been honorably discharged from the police force (flat feet and back pain), refused to join in. The Comandante's picture wasn't up in his home to keep away the president of his local Committee in Defense of the Revolution, but because Usnavy really admired him. Usnavy still volunteered for block-watch duties. He still went down to the Plaza de la Revolución to catch the Comandante's marathon speeches and worked himself into a frenzy of joy, jumping up and down, shouting and waving his little paper flag.

During the Comandante's out-of-town or foreign trips, Usnavy never failed to get to a neighbor's house to watch him on TV. (Years earlier Usnavy had earned the right, through excellence in revolutionary work, to his own television, but to Lidia and Nena's dismay, he'd given it—at the suggestion of a woman from the CDR—to an autistic boy who lived down the street and occasionally hung out at the domino games on Montserrate. "I can't tell who's stupider, you or him," Frank chided him. "The boy's retarded, for god's sake—he can't even tell if the damn thing is on or off.")

In the last few years, Usnavy had served as treasurer of his CDR, making it his duty to gather dues and keep track of project accounts. Most people would have considered it a horrible job—cajoling neighbors and friends, being responsible for almost one hundred pesos a month (sometimes, when somebody was a little short, he'd even put in a few pesos of his own). Yet Usnavy viewed it as an honor, a vote of confidence in his character. It was because of the Revolution, he assured Nena, that he could participate as a responsible member of society, as good as anyone else. It was because of the Revolution, he believed, that he wasn't dismissed as some hick from the hills. It was because of the Revolution that the lifeline on his hand had been rerouted, that he was born every day a New Man.

"We're a nation of giants," he'd proclaim, sure that he saw invisible titans marching down the streets, holding up the city, its bridges and towers, factories and monuments.

Which is why, as far as Usnavy was concerned, now that the government had legalized the American dollar in the last year, life had become something of an irony. Obdulio, Diosdado, and Mayito, until recently disillusioned and caustic, were suddenly the happy recipients of legal monthly remittances from their previously treasonous relatives in the U.S. This allowed them to purchase their own color TVs, fresh meat, and comfortable shoes on the black market where Frank was busy earning handsome profits from all sorts of unseemly wheeling and dealing. The rest of the populace verged on the edge of misery.

Usnavy—without relatives abroad to send him dollars, and defiantly refusing to invest or engage in illicit business—didn't know exactly how it all worked, only that his friends were suddenly jovial and that the teasing about his moral rectitude and revolutionary fervor was also at an all-time high. None of their stomachs were churning; none of them lacked the means to buy butter while everyone else ate their bread with salt and vegetable oil.

"Guapón!" Frank gushed, smiling broadly, suggesting Usnavy was even more guapo than the average guapo: a super guapo. Frank slapped him on the back as Usnavy chained his bike to a nearby fence; he flicked the ashes from his cigar.

In reality, Usnavy was thin and gaunt; as he grew older, his previously reddish hair had turned white as sea foam and topped his now sunblotched face. Since his diet had been reduced to rice and, frequently, sugared water for energy during the day, he'd grown even skinnier, with his cheekbones accentuating his face and his fingers long and bony. He knew he had never been handsome, and knew too that, penniless and still steadfast, his friends pitied him too much to think him brave. Guapo, he knew, could just be ironic; indeed, he thought as he took a position in the shade under the tree to watch the game; it probably was something of a jeer.

Frank smirked, threw down a handful of crowded dominos, and declared himself out of the game with a nod toward Usnavy. "Go ahead, guapo, go ahead," he said, surrendering his spot to him. Frank always had a rough but gallant air about him, like the Mexican movie star Anthony Quinn. His departure from the game paired Usnavy with Mayito, the group's best player and Frank's best friend, who liked to keep silent during these informal tournaments. (One of the things Usnavy most liked about dominos was that it was played in teams and required collaboration. But, as far as Usnavy was concerned, to play with Mayito and his silence, you practically had to be a mind reader!)

"Ah, the mute," Usnavy said, a bit reluctantly but still amused. As he settled in across from his wordless partner, it occurred to Usnavy that, in spite of everything, he was content. A bike ride, dominos, his family; it was enough for him.

"Yes, the mute's game," said Frank, nodding in Mayito's direction and lighting a cigar while standing under the tree overlooking the tournament, which was being played on an old card table that wobbled with each turn. The autistic boy to whom Usnavy had given his TV sat stiffly in a nearby chair, staring expressionless at the domino pieces scattered on the tabletop. It was unclear whether he understood that the object of the game was to get rid of one's pieces as quickly as possible; what was certain was that the boy could count. After several outbursts in which he'd given away who had what, or what was still in play, they'd had to threaten to not let him watch in order to get him to keep quiet. Now and then you could still see him moving his lips, but he never spoke anymore, and so the players tolerated him, even grew to think of him as intrinsic to the scene.

At one time, Usnavy's friends had played with one of Gerardo Galbán's beautiful, original bone-and-ebony sets but, in time, the pieces had gotten chipped, then lost, and now they played with a plastic set, black on the back, yellow on the front, brought down from Miami, though rumored to also be made by Galbán himself, now exiled. They had loved to play with that original set, matching the numbers head to head in the light, knowing the pieces would stay put, each game a masterpiece of lines snaking around the table. The problem with the plastic one was that as soon as it got hot and the players began to perspire, the pieces became slippery and would fly out of their hands unexpectedly, or slide out of position at the slightest bump. They had no gravitas. Somebody—usually the autistic boy—had to be watching, making sure the lines were neat and the game was on course.

"I know, I know it's the mute's game," Usnavy said with resignation. "Dominos was invented by a mute, I know." This was a standard introduction to one of Frank's reveries, whether domino-related or not.

"A Chinese mute," Frank affirmed from his perch.

"So now it was the Chinese who invented dominos?" asked Obdulio as he stirred the soup, quickly plucking his ten pieces and lining them up on their sides so they wouldn't tumble. Obdulio was squat and solid, a crown of tight rust-colored curls on his head. "Last week it was the Egyptians."

"See? You're not paying attention," said Frank, letting the cigar smoke out in rings from his mouth like a kid. "I said, the Egyptians played pre-dominos."

Mayito whacked a double nine into the center of the table to start. Diosdado dropped a nine-two next to it, aligning the nines.

"Dolores," Usnavy said, and he meant it: What a pain! He loved to play dominos as much for the commentary as for the game itself. And in this particular group, he was the play-by-play guy, the one who knew what to say after each move, how to name the circumstances of the game.

Dolores really couldn't have been more appropriate: When he finally looked down at his pieces, he had nothing but a bunch of doubles. This was a disastrous hand, the doubles halving his possibilities of matching and connecting. He knew he could have called for a new game—he had more than the five doubles that would have allowed it—but he hadn't been paying attention, didn't call it in time, and understood all too well that to say anything now, after two full plays, was to set himself up for ruthless harassment from Frank not just today but for days to come, maybe weeks.

He tried to cover by placing a nine-seven—one of his few non-doubles—on the other end of the domino tail. "Caracol," he said.

Obdulio put a seven and two in play, leaving both ends of the dominos exposing twos. Frank leaned closer, chewing noisily on his cigar. Mayito, as enigmatic as a Buddha (and just as bald), pushed in a two and six at his near end.

"The Egyptians, I don't know what they played," said Frank, leaning back and taking up his philosophizing again. "It was maybe almost dominos but not quite. That took the genius of the Chinese. Don't you agree, guapo?"

Usnavy was hardly paying attention to him, trying to stay focused on the game. Diosdado, who seemed almost professorial with his bifocals and his thin goatee, had just released a six and four ("Gato," Usnavy grumbled, imagining the four dots as cat's paws) in an effort to see if Usnavy had any twos (he didn't). Usnavy used his only four—the double—and frowned while Obdulio spun a single domino in a playfully threatening fashion next to his hand. He left the domino to whirl and picked another, the four and five. Nobody had touched that two at the other end, except the autistic boy, whose index finger slid it into place when it seemed like it wanted to float away.

The doubles in Usnavy's hand stared up at him, as beautiful and ineffable as feline eyes.

Under the tree, Frank suddenly stopped his story, engaging in a whispered conversation with a greasy young man. Monkish Mayito gave up a two and five, having presumed that his partner was in trouble and trying to give him a way out. But Usnavy was still distracted, watching Frank laughing and exchanging a few dollars for a huge wad of pesos.

That Frank was being so conspicuous was proof of their friendship—and maybe a kind of boast too—but Usnavy couldn't get used to it.

"Hey," Diosdado reproached him, nodding at fives on both ends of the domino trail. To Usnavy, Diosdado seemed even more professor-like at moments like that, when he acted as if he'd caught him daydreaming in class.

"No comment," said Usnavy with a shake of the head. Double five for him, not much choice. Two cats dragging their tails. Mayito's brow arched.

"Ah, yes, the Chinese," Frank said, picking up his story, Cuban bills bulging in his pockets. "You know how they came upon dominos?" He tapped the ashes off his cigar with dramatic flair. Diosdado inched in with a five and eight. "You guys listening? This is important stuff," Frank continued as Usnavy threw down a double eight.

Cats squared. Mayito winced. Obdulio screwed in the eight and two but Mayito came to the rescue with a two and seven.

"Por dios," mumbled Usnavy, and everybody laughed except the autistic boy.

Diosdado left the seven alone; his eyes distorted on the bottom half of his bifocals as he plugged a five and nine on the other end. He was the picture of arrogance, which made Usnavy want to tell him how ridiculous he looked. But he said nothing—why pick a useless fight?—and groaned at his hand, which only brought on more laughter.

"The Chinese used dominos as a way to divine the future," Frank lectured.

Somebody offered Usnavy a thimble of freshly brewed coffee and he downed it. It was bitter and sharp and caused him to grimace involuntarily. Then he tapped the table with his finger, passing.

"Damn, man, you're salao," said the delphic Mayito, meaning the worst kind of unlucky.

"Salao?" asked Frank with a cackle. "My friend here can't be salao—he doesn't believe in that!"

"In what?" asked Diosdado, but he had a little gleam in his eye, making a rare pact with Frank.

"Why, in luck. Usnavy doesn't believe in luck or fate or any of that," Frank continued. "Unless it's the destiny of the whole nation—the ultimate fate of our transcendent Revolution!"

Usnavy was too tired—and this was all such old territory for all of them—to get into any kind of discussion with Frank, with whom no one could ever win. He stared down at his hand and examined the table, noticing how every time Mayito had tried to rescue him by providing connections, the game had turned before it got to him.

"C'mon, c'mon," Diosdado hurried him.

"Well, you're right about one thing," Usnavy said, calling it quits by turning his pieces over, "at least in this game, I'm absolutely salao!"

The group howled, the laughter rising sharp and clear. Every single piece in Usnavy's hand was a double, including the double zero, reflected in the autistic boy's impervious eyes.

A few days later, Usnavy returned to the Old Havana civil registry by himself. There was no point in dragging Nena along, he conceded. Now the walls stood half-painted and a new fluorescent tube hung from the ceiling. The clerk leaned limply against the counter. At Usnavy's insistence, he took down all the information and, after a long, suffocating wait, explained that there wasn't anything he could do for him.

"You need to go to the hospital where she was born," he said with a twitch in his eye. "What we need is the number of her birth certificate."

Usnavy pulled the ruined copy of the original from his pants and searched to see if by chance the numbers might still be decipherable, but neither he nor the clerk could be sure. A weary Usnavy pedaled to work, figuring he'd go to the hospital the next day and take care of the problem.

Maybe, he thought, he should have left Nena out of it from the beginning and taken care of it all by himself.

That evening, before washing up and heading out for his game of dominos, Usnavy watched as Lidia served up a sandwich for Nena that he recognized as having what looked like a reddish-brown meat. His immediate fear was that it was cat flesh. As a delighted Nena ate—complimenting Lidia, savoring the little bits of what looked like onions—Lidia kept busy, avoiding Usnavy's eye. She had not served him a sandwich, only the usual rice with a little bit of black beans. Of all people, of course, he knew that the only ingredient she'd gotten legally for that sandwich was the bread.

"Want a taste, Papi?" Nena offered.

His daughter was a naturally skinny kid, long-limbed and slightly awkward, but he knew that given half a chance she'd grow into her body, that she might even be elegant someday. She had charcoal eyebrows, skin as lustrous and perfect as an apple.

Usnavy shook his head. "Nah, already ate," he muttered. Was she being ironic too? He couldn't tell.

He reached under the bed, next to the piles of books, to the dresser drawer with his clothes, and pulled out a clean pair of underwear. (Lidia and Nena had their own drawer, which was a little bigger.) Usnavy had three pairs and there was a strict cycle to their usage: There was always one on, one drying on the line, and one in the drawer. Lidia and Nena had a few more, four or five each, and they were better at the daily washing than he was so they were never caught off guard. Lidia would have washed his underwear too, but Usnavy had been well-trained by his mother to launder his briefs and undershirts as he bathed, a skill that came in handy during his bachelor years, and which probably helped convince Lidia of his worth as a husband. Usnavy would never be a hero or a star, but he would never be a burden either.

As soon as Nena had finished her meal, she placed her plate in the plastic pan used to soak the dishes, grabbed her toothbrush and the plastic bottle filled with boiled water, then stepped outside. Usnavy could hear her beside the water barrel, brushing and gargling as she greeted passing neighbors.

Lidia handed him a tiny cup of coffee with a head of brown froth. Luckily, she'd drowned the bitterness with enough sugar. "Rosita across the courtyard had a little meat, a little steak she shared with me, in exchange for, you know, the ironing I did for her," Lidia said apologetically.

Often, because Lidia was one of the few people in the world these days with a working iron, they could earn a few extra pesos that way, or barter for goods. The ironing never produced dollars because tourists had their ironing, if any, done at the hotels, and, frankly, neither Usnavy nor Lidia would have known how to approach them anyway.

Now Lidia was fidgeting with the refrigerator, rearranging its meager contents. She was a lean, sienna-skinned woman with narrow hips, younger than Usnavy by a decade, but more fragile. Since Nena's birth, after twenty-two hours in labor, she'd become even shyer than when Usnavy had first met her. Communication seemed like such an effort to her that, as far as Usnavy was concerned, the mere fact that she wanted to explain something made it instantly forgivable, whatever it was. He could barely stand the thought of her discomfort. He sipped his coffee—it was sickly sweet—and handed the cup back to her.

"I thought it was best to give the meat to Nena, but it wasn't very much," Lidia continued. "There really wasn't enough, I didn't even have any myself, just a taste."

Usnavy sat on the bed, quietly tossing his underwear from one hand to the other, like pizza dough. The light from the lamp above them was too bright, the feline eyes like sapphires embedded in their yellow sockets. He noticed a small puddle on the floor, the result of a barely visible but rusty streak that now ran down the wall.

"It's all right, it's all right," he said, embarrassed for both of them. "Don't worry about it."

It was he who was worried, however. He now realized what his little girl had just eaten. Lidia probably wasn't aware that the sandwich she'd bought—he was sure it was not a gift, not an exchange—did not have any meat at all. Most people hadn't figured out the scheme yet but Usnavy was sure he knew the secret behind those tasty treats.

The week before, Rosita had been selling those very sandwiches on the street—she'd even offered him one. But no sooner had Usnavy pulled up the bread and seen the flat layer of pith covered in seasoning, than he recognized its true provenance: These were pieces of a blanket normally used for mopping floors which Rosita had beaten and marinated in spices and a little beef broth. The texture of the wool had been transformed into what they all imagined steak was like, something tender and chewy. The success of her enterprise had come as much from her ingenuity as from the tricks memory plays.

Needless to say, Rosita had sold out of the sandwiches and quickly come back to the bodega to get the blanket due on her mother's ration book. Rosita's excitement that day, he knew, didn't have anything to do with the potential gleam of her floor. Still, he didn't say anything to anyone. Who would believe him anyway? Who would admit they'd been fooled by the sheer force of their desire?

If the enterprise went well enough, he presumed, she'd soon vanish from the bodega's line, acquiring a limitless supply of blankets and dressing from god knows where . . .

The ingredients for the tangy sauce must have been illicitly acquired, Usnavy mused after a minute—and his daughter had just eaten it with pieces of wool. At least it wasn't cat meat, he thought.

Then he bowed his head in dismay and disbelief.

A few nights later, Usnavy and his family were startled by a thunderous rapping on the door of their room. Both Lidia and Nena shot up, Nena reaching with her foot to the cot where her father lay to poke him awake. His mattress was thin and spread on top of a layer of old *Granma* newspapers that crinkled when he moved (*Granma*, in English, after the boat the rebels took from Mexico to Cuba to spark the Revolution).

"Usnavy," came the hoarse whisper from outside. "Usnavy, please, I need your help."

Usnavy felt his way to the door in the darkness, cracking it open a sliver. Outside, there were only shadows but he recognized the tight curls on the head of his friend Obdulio, squat and solid, standing there nervously.

"Usnavy, you've got to help me," Obdulio said.

"What happened?"

"Everybody's leaving," he said.

Last spring, a few people had jumped the fence at the Belgian embassy and Obdulio had said the same thing: *Everybody's leaving*—but it wasn't to be. And then in a matter of weeks, there were nearly a dozen Cubans in the Chilean embassy and a bunch who smashed through the fence with a truck at the German mission, all waiting for the authorities to relent and give them a way out of Cuba. But after weeks of delays, they all trickled back to the streets of Havana, hungrier and more distraught than ever. And in spite of the risks and the drama, nobody left.

"What do you mean?" asked a groggy Usnavy. He was shirtless, standing in the doorway in his underwear. The floor was wet and slippery and the sour smell of the tenement invaded his nostrils. By now both Lidia and Nena were beside him wrapped in the bed sheet.

"In Cojímar, it's like Mariel," Obdulio said, swallowing hard.

Usnavy felt both Lidia and Nena tense up next to him. "What does that have to do with me?" he asked wearily.

Not again, he thought, not again. Back in 1980, during the leakage from Mariel harbor, how many had left? How many had disappeared? How many had never been heard from again?

"I'm leaving," Obdulio said. "My family and I, we're leaving. We're building a raft right now, my daughter and my nephews. They're already there, on the beach."

"You've thought about this?" asked Usnavy, turning in to his family's room.

"Yes, yes, of course," Obdulio said. He pushed his way inside, forcing Nena to scramble up on the bed to make room. "Look, Usnavy, you need to think about it too. What are you doing here, my friend?"

"What would I do *there?*" he asked.

"Anything!" said Obdulio. "Anything's better than here! You don't have to be salao forever."

Usnavy reached up for the cord to turn on the magnificent lamp.

There in the flood of light was an anxious, blinking Lidia and an eager Nena, both staring at him.

"Usnavy, we have room, we have room for all of you," Obdulio said.

Usnavy shook his head. "I like it here."

"You like it here? Usnavy, this is me you're talking to!" Obdulio implored. "Usnavy, people are leaving on any piece of plastic that'll float. Remember the guy who flew the crop duster all the way to Key West? Or—wait!—when all those American pastors came, the people near the harbor trying to get a little box of crackers or a can of soup? What do you think that was about, my friend? You think you're immune?"

"Those people, they were a disgrace, begging like that!" Usnavy insisted. As he spoke, he couldn't help but notice how Lidia's thin shoulders dropped and how Nena quietly curled into a ball on the bed and turned her face to the wall. She held on to the corner of the sheet, smudged and sopping from the floor now, which barely covered her.

"They were a disgrace," he repeated, hoping to elicit a different reaction from his wife and daughter.

"Lidia, talk to him," Obdulio pleaded.

Lidia nodded, standing there with the rest of the bed sheet around her, but kept her silence.

"I'm sorry," Usnavy said. "I'm grateful to you for thinking of us, for your good intentions, but . . ."

Obdulio abruptly grabbed the door and slammed it shut. "Okay, fine, stay," he said. "Rot if you like."

Usnavy shrugged. "Look, you're doing better than most, with all those dollars you're getting from your brother, and the ones you're making here doing whatever . . ."

"I'll make more there," Obdulio said.

Usnavy nodded. "Probably, probably."

"Look, stay or go, you have to help me anyway, you have to get me some supplies. I need rope, I need some powdered milk."

"Obdulio . . . I . . ."

"What? You can't get me some lousy rope and milk? My daughter is taking the baby!" Obdulio was getting agitated.

Usnavy looked around the room, at his frightened wife and daughter. "I'm not going to discuss this here, Obdulio," he said, pushing his friend out the door.

Then he pulled on his trousers and a T-shirt, grabbed his bike, and followed Obdulio out into the night.

The two men arrived in Cojímar hours later but while it was still dark. They'd ridden to the beach on their Flying Pigeon bikes, manual and heavy, made in China in spite of the English name.

"The Chinese can divine the future but they can't make a lightweight bike?" a gasping Obdulio muttered, the curls on his head uncoiling in the breeze, looking now like loose pieces of a dirty sponge.

The ride to Cojímar was always against the wind. Usnavy kept pedaling. Because there was no transportation in the middle of the night—the bus that ferried bikes to the city stopped sometime after dusk—and because non-motorized vehicles were strictly prohibited through the Havana Tunnel, they'd had to go around the bay, adding even more time to their journey. Usnavy wore a lock and chain around his waist to tie his bike but Obdulio had clipped to his a nifty, lightweight U-shaped lock, solid steel and made in the U.S., guaranteed theft-proof. (No doubt a gift from his exiled brother, Usnavy figured.)

They entered the cozy fishing village as a silent parade of young men and women made a line to the shore. Carrying inner tubes and wooden planks, they looked like rows of giant ants hauling Lifesavers and tooth-picks in the moonlight. Watching it all from the protected confines of elegant Las Terrazas—one of Ernest Hemingway's old haunts—were foreign tourists, their giggles bubbling in the air, and journalists too, TV camera lights washing the landscape. (Also somewhere in the restaurant: Gregorio Fuentes, Hemingway's old boat captain, now practically mummified, propped up to play checkers or dominos for the tourists' delight.)

Near the rocky shore—Cojímar is all dog's teeth, a snarling bank of coral and junk—groups of people hammered away at their rafts, tying ropes around pieces of rubber, metal kegs, and plastic jugs for buoyancy. There were no surfboards anywhere, no windsurfers pretending science or recreation. This was all out in the open; the Revolution suspended.

A different group stood apart from the builders, waiting, not so much for the rafts to be built but for other, northern sailors: These folks, dressed for holiday travel—some carrying suitcases, umbrellas, a bowler hat or two, still others with plastic bags or bundles wrapped in newspapers, others nothing at all—gazed at the black waters, watching for the flicker of faraway flares, ready at a moment's notice to leave behind even those very satchels that now seemed so precious, and leap onto whatever gleaming white yacht or slick flat cigarette boat kissed the shore. Although some had flashlights, and others hurricane lamps lit by who knows what for fuel, everyone was featureless except for their eyes: large white orbs, slightly startled by the sudden bursts of light.

On this night, different from every other night in Usnavy's memory, the town sloped down to the sea but he labored to envision instead plateaus and rugged ranges. In his mind, he was somewhere else: Ka-tanga or Shaba, an impenetrable forest full of wild geese and ostriches, buffalo, and lions. He imagined not rafters but fields of coffee and cotton; rubber trees, coconut, and plantain; timber from cedar, mahogany, iroko, and redwood. The staring eyes were the peacocks Usnavy had never seen, pelicans, herons, and other wild birds.

While the work continued on the beach, no one said a word except the local fishermen, who held tightly to their rolls of lines and gaffs, nets and tattered masts. Their own boats securely put away or anchored under guard, they sat vigilantly on the seawall, their arms across their chests, sucking on cigars and hand-rolled cigarettes, passing judgment on the work before them. One guy tapped a long hardwood stick on the ground, another held a machete against his hip in a not so subtle warning to potential thieves. Not far from them, a few boys rolled dice against the seawall, occasionally shouting with victory.

"That won't go, no," said an old man in a red cap, pointing to a particularly chancy-looking homemade dinghy. The others nodded agreement.

"That's unbalanced too—look at that," a second fisherman said as he singled out another one. "They'll roll right into the water in that, you watch."

"Qué va," exclaimed yet another fellow, shaking his head in dismay at a throng of young men and women who were now lifting what looked like a white wooden kayak. They carried it to the water, where it swayed on the surface. As soon as one of the young men stepped into it, his weight took it down as if it were made of paper. A collective moan went up from the group, while they quickly scrambled to recover what they could from the ocean and start again. The fishermen laughed and laughed.

Some of the rafts, of course, did float. Some precariously, others effortlessly. Usnavy listened to the dip and push of their efforts as the moon sank from sight.

In a clearing, Usnavy finally saw the boat being crafted by Obdulio's family, which was dependent on four large industrial inner tubes—Usnavy didn't want to know where they'd gotten them. Obdulio's nephews secured the craft tighter with the length of rope Usnavy had procured for them. Like the others, Obdulio's nephews didn't speak, only nodded their appreciation. Obdulio's daughter thanked Usnavy for the powdered milk with a quick, timid peck on the cheek. The baby was fast asleep on her shoulder, undisturbed by the bustle of activity.

Usnavy moved quickly away from them. He did not want to look at the rope; he did not want to consider the powdered milk. Before he'd gathered them up, the rope had belonged to the workers of Cuba; the milk had been for the island's children. (As crazy as it seemed, he really believed this; his heart twisted in anguish because he *so* believed this.) He let himself replay the scene at the bodega, watched himself as if he were someone else, carefully lifting the rope and powdered milk his dear friend needed, knowing he could not replace them, knowing that everything was wrong now, everything was ugly and sick.

That he loved Obdulio and his family was not the matter; after all, it was Che himself who said that a true revolutionary is guided by great feelings of love. That he loved them so much that he put them above everyone else—that was the black smear on his soul now. Usnavy's hands trembled, his eyes moistened from shame.

How—he was asking himself, his hands deep in his empty pockets—how could he ever question anyone else? How could he ever seek out the answers to other missing items at the bodega, rice and soap and cooking oil that were sometimes reduced by half from arrival to dispensing? What about the blankets that someone would no doubt steal for Rosita? He would never—not with a clear conscience, not without first confessing his own transgression—be able to ask that the others be mindful and disciplined, that they be selfless in their duties. He could see his coworkers shrinking from him. Or worse: What if they suddenly included him in their schemes? What if his crime automatically implicated him in every other petty theft at the bodega? What if, once revealed, he was expected to cover for everyone else so that they'd cover for him?

Usnavy shuddered. He thought of Lidia for a moment, worried about what her response would be. His stomach flipped, made him a little seasick. He stepped back from the water.

"In Miami," said Obdulio, now beside him and gazing out at the gloom before them, "maybe I'll finally learn to drive a car."

"You could learn to drive here," Usnavy replied, thinking how it had never really been essential.

Until recently, buses had been plentiful, distances all seemed attainable. At the end of her cab route, Lidia, herself a bus driver's daughter, had always come home energized, ready for more. (She would have been a bus driver too, if only she'd had the opportunity.) Usnavy had learned to drive long ago, back in Oriente, when he was only fifteen. It was a strange feeling, all that power in his hands, though none of it ever truly his: Each time he drove, it was with a burly American who'd sit next to him, or frolic with a local in the backseat while he toured the lesser-known roads aimlessly.

"Nobody's stopping you," Usnavy finally said.

Obdulio sighed. "Yeah, but what for? And in whose car? I'll never get to own a car here. Neither will you, my militant friend."

"You think you'll get a car there? Do you have any idea how much a car costs?" Usnavy asked.

"No, but my brother . . . he has a car and, god willing, I'll get to drive it."

"Seems like a stupid reason to leave . . ."

"C'mon, Usnavy . . . don't you have any aspirations? Don't you want a place to live that's made for humans instead of laboratory mice? Don't you want a little privacy with your wife? Don't you have any dreams?"

"This is my dream," Usnavy said.

He stepped away again, watching as another group labored over planks and tubes, but Obdulio moved right along with him. Usnavy wanted to say something—anything—so they wouldn't go. He wondered how many would disappear like his own father, gone without a trace into the blue.

Obdulio persisted. "C'mon . . . when you look at that crazy lamp of yours—do you realize it's the only thing you have of value, my friend? Don't you see anything in all that light and color besides clouds and giraffes and Africa? Africa—I mean, Usnavy, how perverse is that? Who dreams of Africa when you can dream of Miami? Don't you see any hope at all?"

Usnavy took a deep breath. "Obdulio, I am here because you are my friend," he said. "Now I will ask you to be a friend to me and stop this crap. I'm not leaving, now or ever."

Obdulio shrugged. "Fine," he said as his nephews began to drag their raft to the water. It eased in with squeaks and whines, bouncing on the soft waves with the weight of each new person. Usnavy took off his shoes and socks and stepped into the sea to help, the smell of saline almost overwhelming him. He held onto the raft and steadied it as they loaded up, all the while feeling the sharp rocks under his feet, the ticklish weeds wrapping themselves around his ankles. The local fishermen looked on, nodding approval at the superior work. Finally, it was Obdulio's turn to board.

"Look, your wife and daughter . . . Usnavy, you need to get over this saintly devotion, your ridiculously selfish virtues," Obdulio said, one foot on the gravelly sand, the other on the shaky vessel. "If you're going to stay, for god's sake, at least do something for them . . . get some dollars. If you sell that lamp—it's a monstrosity, it must be worth at least a few hundred, maybe even a thousand dollars!—think of what you can do. You could start your own little business on the side, you could buy things Nena and Lidia only dream about."

Obdulio's daughter took his hand to help him sit, and with a bereft Usnavy waist deep in the water, the raft pushed off.

"Good luck," Usnavy said, waving weakly.

"Good luck to you, my friend," Obdulio shot back.

The raft glided away, pulled north by the currents. Its shadow clung to the shore at first, black figures thinning, then turning into gold strings reaching back to the island. As he watched, Usnavy discerned the arcs of flying fish in the distance, like pebbles skipping across the surface. He felt something collapse in his chest. This was it, he realized with a start, this was the last time he'd ever see his lifelong friend.

In a moment, Obdulio's raft had vanished into the bright nimbus of dawn.

The trip home from Cojímar was usually easier, downhill with the wind in the biker's favor, but this time it was longer. Usnavy couldn't count the hours; they seemed so viscid and unreal. Part of the difficulty was that Obdulio had left his bike as a gift for Nena—Usnavy knew she'd be thrilled—and he was having difficulty maneuvering both bikes at once. He'd tried riding his and leading the other with one hand on the handlebars, but the roads around the bay to Havana were demolished, as if a squadron of bombers had just passed, and what had been inconvenient zigzagging en route to Cojímar had become impossible on the way home. The two times a truck zoomed by, it knocked Usnavy off balance. Then his feet began to hurt; taking off his shoes and socks to get in the sea and help push off Obdulio's raft had exposed his bare soles to the craggy reefs. Not only had he been cut, bitten, and scratched in a million places, but his joints ached and his skin itched from the dried salt.

To make things worse, as soon as Usnavy decided against trying to ride and surrendered to walking home holding a bike on each side, it began to rain. A rush of water soaked him from the tip of his head to the squishy toes of his now surely ruined shoes. The downpour grew so intense that Usnavy couldn't see anything but a gray mist in front of him. It fell with all the noisy fury of a galloping herd of horses, tiny hoofs rampaging all over his exposed skin.

There was no point in running for cover; the shower had come after an ear-splitting crack in the sky, as if it had abruptly opened up, sending a cascade from the heavens to this caiman of dirt. Usnavy wondered about Obdulio and his family. Would they survive the storm? Might they be just out of its reach, or were they now bailing water out of the boat, desperate and scared?

Maybe, thought Usnavy, turning the matter over, the weight of so many Cuban prayers had finally eroded celestial resistance. (He was an inadvertent believer, his faith so personal and spontaneous that it stood apart from all debate about the merits of religion, or even his own conscious acknowledgment.) Maybe, he pondered, the layer of sky that works as a streambed had been undermined, finally giving way and discharging into a divine cataract.

This is Mosi-oa-Tunya—Victoria Falls—he mused, as the water plunged from hundreds of feet above him with a mighty howl and pounded on his shoulders and back. If only this could be harvested somehow, if only Cuba could absorb this awesome force. (It would solve all the electrical problems, that's for sure.) It was coming down in a furious free fall.

A drenched Usnavy was limping along when he thought he saw a shadowy shape—something eerie, its limbs oversized, its head sprouting a kind of feathery ornament. Was it one of his giants, one of those Goliaths on whom he was sure the entire city was dependent? Usnavy stared ahead as the shape slipped right through the screen of water in front of him. He stopped, leaned a bike against each hip, and ran a hand over his face. But when he looked up again, he saw not one but several black stick figures sneaking in and out of view in the blink of an eye.

As Usnavy stared ahead, he realized they'd begun to take notice of him too: He was sure one had just made a quick gesture his way, pointing and snapping its fingers; another clicked its tongue. Usnavy shook his head like a dog that's just made it back to shore, trying to regain composure. Then he looked again: There they were, the figures now more roundly human, less black and more muddled, rushing in and out of the undulating sheets of rain. There were voices too, each mixed into the soundtrack of thunder and the rattle of water on the pavement, nearby awnings, and cars.

Somebody somewhere was playing with sticks, their *tick tock* marking the time. There was a flicker of light, a flash. Instantly Usnavy realized he was in Old Havana, right on Tejadillo, only blocks from home.

"Cuida'o, abuelo, cuida'o," a young man called out as he snaked around Usnavy.

He was carrying long pieces of wood, their ends jagged as if they'd been torn. Usnavy pulled back, avoiding the spear points by centimeters.

"Ojo, ojo," called out another man as he dashed by—almost running into him—pushing a wheelbarrow full of bricks still covered with paint and mortar. The chalky stench of wet plaster rose like vapor.

"Usnavy!" a woman shouted, but with an unmistakable tone of annoyance. "For god's sake, you're in the way!"

It was, he noticed, his upstairs neighbor, shamelessly reaping construction materials from the ruins of the building next to him—a derrumbe that had suddenly come in to view. The building lay like a crushed egg, parts of its white walls piercing the exposed insides: a smashed mirror, a stained mattress ripped open like a vital organ, its yellow foam guts growing grotesquely in the rain.

"Yamilet, what's going on?" Usnavy called out to her. "What are you doing?"

She rushed by him with doorknobs and light switches dangling from her hands like viscera. "What does it look like?"

It looked, Usnavy thought, like a scourge of locusts. His neighbors swarmed the body of the place, each tearing off bits that seemed two or three times their size and weight. They worked like the rafters at Cojímar, in utter silence. The only sound came from rocks groaning as they were moved, the hard human breathing of such extraordinary effort, and the occasional mumbled courtesy or warning extended a bystander such as himself.

In a moment, Usnavy realized he was drip-drying, the rain having stopped abruptly, the warmth slowly returning to his face and shoulders. He felt the water still on him running down, inexorably pulled by the magic of gravity. It clung to the bottom edges of his T-shirt, the rim of his short sleeves, and the seams of his pants. The rest of his clothing stiffened a bit as if touched by a natural starch.

Usnavy looked up—it was only mid-morning and the sun, though rising, wasn't quite high enough to hide the beauty of a western rainbow, its red arch sweeping across the colonial rooftops. He located the orange, yellow, and green layers that dropped down—like on his own lamp at home—and then just below the first rainbow, a second, paler one, barely visible, like the reflection in his own amazed eyes.

To his surprise, Usnavy spotted a glint of the same swatch of colors in the earthly rubble before him, now stripped clean of every usable element. He leaned forward and squinted, holding onto the handlebars of the bikes on either side of him, trying to make out exactly what it was. Everyone seemed to be walking away now; no one else appeared to care or even notice the tiny fountain of colors. Yet the beams danced and danced: ruby, gold, emerald.

With the bikes at his sides, Usnavy pulled up as close as he could to the edge of the wreckage, but he was still too far to decipher the precise secret of the light in the ruins. With luck, he thought, he might be able to maneuver the bikes over there. But after venturing a bit in to the destruction site, it became clear that was impossible: There were rusted nails poking out everywhere, broken cement, sharp rocks, slippery puddles of rain. The tires wouldn't make it; the chains might get caught on something. And the bikes were so heavy.

Again Usnavy leaned on the bikes and stretched forward for a closer look, but the shards of color sparkled obliquely. He wondered if perhaps his eyes were playing tricks on him. He'd heard on the streets how the food shortages had begun taking their toll on people, how the new spartan diets had started to eat at some, making their bones mushy, causing paralysis and blindness in others.

Usnavy rubbed his eyes, looked again. Then, to be sure he wasn't imagining anything, he pulled a coin—a hollow Cuban coin—out of his pocket and pitched it in the direction of the shiny treasure. The coin struck something, producing a little geyser of what looked like red mist or powder.

Usnavy was taken aback. He put the bikes down in a pile, Obdulio's newer one on top so it wouldn't get scratched, and rather than undo the chain around his waist and deal with that complication, he snapped the American U-shaped lock on the necks of both bikes so that they seemed to be embracing. He dashed to the lights, skipping over chunks of broken walls, rusted steel spokes, shredded paperback books, and the inevitable orange slush from the old building's life fluids.

The lights! Usnavy got down on his knees. The lights came from a lamp like his, only small, injured, its stained-glass panels fractured, strings of soft mucilage barely holding onto a piece of glass here, a loose wire there. Usnavy unearthed the heavy brass base, shoved aside the pieces of cement that pinned it, and held the lamp, letting light filter through its surviving color insets, the rainbow passing through to his face and chest.

Instantly, he felt the light waves oscillating somewhere deep inside him. At that moment, Usnavy could surrender to the splendor; he could believe, like Pythagoras, that everything could become bright by its own force of nature.

Light! Light!—marveled Usnavy, there on his knees, the lamp lifted to the heavens—the closest thing to infinite speed, a mystery to Plato and Euclid, Alhazen and even Einstein.

There was a commotion somewhere behind him but Usnavy was enraptured: The light swarmed around him, lapped at his face and shoulders.

"Usnavy! Usnavy!" came the screams.

He turned around in time to see his neighbor Yamilet running wildly after the two bikes, miraculously unhinged from the theft-proof American lock and whirling down the narrow streets. The bandits were two young men, their long hair tousled like action movie stars, one of them wearing a Chicago Bulls jersey. They laughed and disappeared into the maze of Old Havana, while Yamilet and a gaggle of kids trailed behind them yelling insults and profanities in their direction.

"Shame on you, you bastards, you're stealing from a harmless old man!" she shouted at them.

A flabbergasted Usnavy stood alone in the middle of the collapse, the broken lamp in his hands while the American lock mocked him from a muddy puddle, gleaming like new, its tiny key still embedded in the slot. Had the simplicity of it confused him? Had he been so distracted . . . ?

"Of all the rotten . . . !" Usnavy burst, kicking the lock against a shattered wall, stomping through the building's remnants and accidentally ripping and loosening the sole of his right shoe. The lock bounced away, unharmed, the key like a bell's clapper.

"Salao! Salao! Salao!" he ranted, hitting the air, booting rocks and debris all about the ruins.

Yamilet watched, stunned, as an exhausted Usnavy finally dropped to the ground, folding himself into a filthy fetus, a kaleidoscope of light in his bloody hands.

II.

F **or days afterward, Usnavy strolled** like a tourist through Old Havana—
looking up at the buildings as if for the first time—his eyes searching
for the dazzle of color he'd found in the lamp in the ruins. He'd peek
between the arms and legs of the invisible giants that held up the city;
through the unlit frames of balconies, the tall bars on the windows, the
iron balustrades, searching for the spark that indicated the possibility
that, somewhere inside, there was another nugget of color—a flame, a
spark, a rainbow burst.

In the library he looked in dusty magazines and catalogues from
before the Revolution and studied the lamps: avatars of modernism,
designed for electricity, so popular in Cuba precisely for those reasons.
After all, the Cubans—in this case blessed instead of cursed by U.S.
intervention—had electricity before most of the American South and
other rural areas. But, to Usnavy's chagrin, there was that constant
confusion of the U.S. and modernity, as if living in the twentieth century
were inextricably tied to the island's northern neighbor, an undercurrent
more powerful than any storm. To have an electric lamp in Cuba in the
Republic's early years didn't just mean comfort or affluence, it meant an
implied intimacy with the colossus of the north.

Usnavy closed a catalogue he had been examining and flipped
through some old issues of *Bohemia* magazine instead. There were

stained-glass lamps in those too, depicted in ads and illustrations, dropping from the ceilings of mansions, at the elbow of a banker at his desk, or with the banker's wife, posed with a floor model for the society pages. Usnavy set the magazine down and ran his fingers through his hair. There was only so much he could absorb, only so much he could take in without feeling his stomach grow queasy and his hands begin to tremble.

After a few hours of trying to understand the lamp—the little lamp, the injured one he'd brought home from the derrumbe—he set himself on a route through Old Havana, scoping out the possibilities of finding another small and simple thing. If he could get some glass to match that of his find, he could figure out later how to cut it and work it into the frame (which needed to be straightened out and reinforced).

Often, though, what he spied instead were vitrales—those stained-glass portals above doors or windows—usually drawn like petals or blossoms, but in primary reds and blues, yellows and nebulous white. They were very pretty, he thought, but a little vulgar, certainly not gorgeous like his magnificent lamp, or even the injured one, with their tight, meticulous designs, their colors like dawn or the many shades the sea boasts when it nestles against the coast.

The purpose of the vitrales, he realized, was exactly the opposite of that of the lamps. Instead of delivering light, the vitrales were designed to temper its intensity. They were part of the eighteenth-century criollo architects' scheme—with impossibly high ceilings, top-to-bottom windows, fluttering shutters—to create dark little rooms, cool and dry, a refuge from the heat and daze of the tropics. Instead of cradling its inhabitants in a homey shade, criollo architecture obliterated any notion of privacy and left them as exposed as nomads on the Sahel, victims to every climatic extreme. The floor-to-ceiling windows were essentially doors with bars, allowing anyone on the streets to put a spotlight on life inside at any time: a young woman doing the wash in a metal tub, kids reading imported comic books, a circle of seniors playing mah-jongg.

The tall rooms usually opened up to a central patio ringed by a balcony that served as both perch and thoroughfare. Without hall-ways, the tenants used these terraces to navigate from room to room. But when it rained or stormed, they became wet and slippery, forcing the residents inside, knocking from bedroom door to bedroom door, tiptoeing around weeping widows in moments of prayer, embarrassed young lovers, or harried mothers hoping for a moment of quiet.

Now here he was, suddenly a voyeur, contributing to the spectacle: eyeing every flash of light in each humble home, sticking his nose be-tween the window bars to see if he could spy a lamp inside, even talking up old women (and some young ones too, who surely thought him an amusing old man, not lecherous but eccentric), just to find out if there were more of these lamps somewhere out there and what he could learn from them. Instinctively, Usnavy refrained from talking to men—the few who might hang out at home during the thermal afternoons—afraid they might see through him, all the way to his newly emerging and em-barrassing cupidity.

"Oh, yes, they're American, the lamps you're talking about," said an elderly woman with a kindly grandmother's face. They were talking through the bars on her window, like courting teenagers. She was jittery in all her extremities, mahogany-colored. Usnavy imagined her ances-tors tender and sweet, among the thousands of outwitted, unwilling seafarers at Badagry or Gorée more than a century ago.

"Excellent lamps, excellent—as only Americans can make them," she continued.

She lived only blocks from Usnavy, though it seemed a universe away. He was sure he'd spotted a large auspicious shape above her shoulder, a muted aurora. "They're for kings and presidents, you know, for kings and presidents . . ."

"Kings and presidents?" Usnavy asked with a laugh as he tried to focus on what appeared to be an extraordinary shade draped in shadow above a table in a back room. One of the rear walls seemed to be tilting.

"Yes, every palace has one—every palace in every country. Somebody told me that. I mean, in civilized countries," the old woman went on.

"Every one?" he asked, making time, wondering why he'd never noticed that before, curious as to how it might look blazing with light: Would it be like his? Would it shout out its colors? Was it even more resplendent?

"Well, maybe they're not for kings and presidents anymore," the elderly woman said, distracted by Usnavy's fixed look over her shoulder. There seemed to be a quiet, powdery burst now and again from her ceiling, a little shower of dust that rained down on her. "But they're very nice, very elegant, don't you think?"

Usnavy nodded, then swabbed his sweaty face with his forearm. It was so hot his feet were swelling.

"We have . . . I mean, we had one once, a very big one, massive, but then it broke, and—" She stopped; to Usnavy she was clearly reconsidering what she was about to say. "You know, I think my grandson took it . . ."

She said she didn't know what he'd done with the lamp, of course, and it had been so many years . . . In fact, her grandson was now in Miami, the prosperous owner of a Ford dealership, selling updated versions of those rumpling metal hulks that somehow managed to get gasoline in spite of the shortages and then slowly paraded down the Malecón.

"See them? They're forty, fifty years old and they're still going," she said about the old Fords, successfully changing the subject, "unlike all those other ones . . ." She didn't finish her sentence but Usnavy understood: She meant the Ladas, the Volgas, far newer but lying like clubbed seals on the sides of the roads.

"You know my washing machine?" she asked. "It's prehistoric, a crocodile, but it works. It's a Kenmore, a Sears. See what I mean?"

Usnavy nodded quietly. Why were these the only kinds of conversations he seemed to be having lately? He didn't want to argue. Besides, what was there to argue about? He had never handled any of those appliances long enough to know anything about them, whether they were made in California or China. And what he knew about washing clothes, besides the necessary pressure to clean certain stains, was that—after thirty-five years of Revolution and scores of imported allied laundry detergent as well as the occasional domestic product—everybody still referred to the powdery stuff as Fab, as if they couldn't shake the long northern shadow even in matters as simple as that.

Usnavy scowled without meaning to. His hands still stung from the cuts he'd gotten rescuing the injured lamp in the derrumbe. And now he had a burgeoning blister on his foot from so much walking. He realized that, even as they spoke, the woman's grandson might well be selling a big whale of a Ford to Obdulio right then and there.

And here he was in the meantime, meandering through the old neighborhood in a stupor of afternoon light, the sole of his right shoe sewn back on by his neighbor, Jacinto, with fibers pulled from a piece of the rope he'd taken—he still couldn't get over it: he'd stolen—for Obdulio's fateful trip. What the hell was wrong with him?

As Usnavy turned home at the cathedral plaza, his mind still on the

Badagry woman, a group of young people gathered to sing Christian songs.

"Let there be light!" one of them shouted with exaggerated glee. By his red singed nose and accent Usnavy knew right away he was an American missionary, there to save their sweltering souls.

"Genesis 1:3!" shouted a young Cuban convert, smiling with pride at his rudimentary knowledge. The others clapped approvingly, deferring.

"What light?" Usnavy said, suddenly angry.

He wasn't usually one to inject himself into public discussions but these people were just steps from his home, and getting closer every day. Hanging out with Frank during his years of Quaker schooling and subsequent disillusionment, Usnavy had learned a few things. Later, when Frank joined a Baptist group that had Bible classes every Wednesday night, he brought Usnavy and the other boys those lessons too. Diosdado would read over the controversial passages so he could respond to Frank. Usnavy had learned much about the Bible by listening to them argue.

"God didn't create the sun, the moon, or the stars until the fourth day!" Usnavy yelled at the missionaries. "Haven't you gotten that far? So what light, huh? It defies logic, doesn't it—even its own internal logic?" He smirked, he snarled.

The Cuban faces went blank and turned to the foreign teacher.

"Brother, don't be so angry," said the American, but in a conciliatory, calm tone. He had thin, stringy hair, eyes that seemed transparent. His Spanish was a long slur but the Cubans sighed, so enraptured were they with him. "The answer is right in the Bible, in Isaiah 30:26: 'The light of the sun shall be sevenfold, as the light of the seven days.' See, brother, the light of creation was seven times brighter than the sun!"

Usnavy was aghast. "What . . . ?"

The light of creation was brighter than the sun? How could that be? (Why—*why*—did these people always have an answer? Why were they always so damn sure of themselves? At moments like these, he utterly loathed them—and felt justified in his disdain, leaning again on Che: "A people without hatred cannot vanquish a brutal enemy.")

"This is an opiate," a flustered Usnavy said, falling back on the quickest argument he could conjure, the only response in which he felt safe. "He's brainwashing you!" he exclaimed to his fellow Cubans as he pointed at the foreigner and swiftly walked away. He could feel the pilgrims' gaze burning beatifically on his fading figure, their prayers aimed like missiles at his savage soul.

The small, wounded lamp needed parts. It needed a few new glass inserts, some soldering; the neutered base, with its sculpted bronze, begged for polishing. Usnavy had used his silk cloth as best he could, but the lamp required more than elbow grease. He'd examined its skeleton and figured he could get any welding that might be necessary done somewhere, but he needed to find the colored glass pieces to fit into it first.

Like some of the lamps he'd seen that held glass between copper foil—one at a dollar-only restaurant, another long ago at the home of the poet Regino Boti, back in his youth in Guantánamo—the little injured one varied from the magnificent one at home, which was held together with a lead armature. Instead of feline eyes, the small one was dominated by a dragonfly motif. He figured there had to be others like it; indeed, he had a gut feeling that the Badagry woman was holding out or just plain lying to him: How would her grandson sneak such a lamp out of the country? And why? The whole idea was preposterous. He'd have to question her about it further next time.

After days seeking her out—and learning she had two widowed sisters who also lived with her—he was growing impatient. Her windows and doors were shut whenever Usnavy made his way to and from work. When he asked about her, the neighbors shrugged, surprised that he hadn't found her or one of her sisters at home. They seemed amazed that the sisters were so difficult for him to locate. After a few days, they began to eye him suspiciously, so that Usnavy realized he'd have to develop a different approach, he'd have to think more on how to engage Badagry or her sisters, how to win their trust so he could get invited in and examine the lamp for himself. After all, if their lamp had glass like his little one, it could solve a lot of problems. And Usnavy was only too happy to imagine them sharing in whatever he could procure for a fixed and shiny new lamp, no matter how modest. That was his way; whatever was available was for everyone equally.

That was what he knew and understood.

A few days later, on a whim, he decided to visit Lámparas Cubanas, a factory not far from his neighborhood that had been around long before the Revolution. After the collapse of the socialist bloc, the shop had fallen on hard times—like everything else in Cuba—but Usnavy had heard that in the last year a Portuguese investor had entered the picture and he'd noticed activity again. Perhaps he could get parts there (and then he wouldn't have to depend on Badagry or on scavenging), or at least find out where they might be available.

Lámparas Cubanas was a dingy place, anonymous from the outside. The entranceway had the grimy look of neglect. There were handprints on the wall, the unguinous traces of too many cigarettes, and the empty feel of boredom. Instead of showing off the factory's own products, a fluorescent tube flickered on the ceiling, naked and white.

The moment the young fellow at the battered front desk saw Usnavy trudging in with the injured lamp, he seemed dubious—less about the lamp than about Usnavy himself. "We don't do repairs," he sniffed. "And we only work for hotels and restaurants."

"Yes, yes," Usnavy said as humbly as possible. "I was thinking, though, you could refer me to someone or some place that fixes lamps like this because, well, normally I repair everything myself but this—as you can see—this is a special lamp. I'm not sure my meager talents are up to it. That's why I came here, because I figured you must be experts."

The clerk eyed him skeptically but Usnavy refused to understand that he was supposed to leave, the lamp cradled in his arms like a wounded animal.

"Does the electricity on it work?" the clerk asked after Usnavy delicately deposited it on the desk. The clerk stood up, lighting a cigarette, and leaned against the stained wall, ignoring the display area to the side (closed off by locked mustard-colored gates that made the lamps—spider-armed pieces, torcheries, chandeliers, sconces, table lamps—all seem like prisoners).

"I . . . I don't know about the electricity," Usnavy said. He'd forgotten all about that.

The young man looked at him incredulously. "You mean you didn't check?" He was in his early twenties, wearing a tight-fitting surely imported-from-Miami green Polo shirt, muscular underneath despite the shortages. Whenever he moved—out of obligation or indignation—he seemed to be taking on poses from the old Robert De Niro movies that were broadcast on government TV Saturday nights.

"Well, I . . ." Usnavy began.

"What is it, a Tiffany? A LaFarge? A Murano? Is there a foreigner who wants to buy it?" the impatient clerk asked. He dragged dramatically on his cigarette.

Usnavy glanced around nervously. "No, no, of course not . . ."

A foreigner! A week ago—before Obdulio's departure, before the bike theft, before Nena's soft weeping in the middle of the night—the suggestion would have flustered him because of its illicit implications, but now it had him positively shivering because of the prospects.

"But . . . eh . . . do you—do you know a foreigner who might want to buy it?" he clumsily asked the young man. Even at that moment, Usnavy couldn't believe his own words and his hand flew to his mouth, his fingertips trembling with remorse. Maybe the clerk could direct him to the Portuguese businessman who'd saved the factory.

The brawny boy ignored him and bent over the lamp. "Let me see something," he said, examining the base, which Usnavy considered the least interesting part. For a moment, as the clerk bowed his head, showing Usnavy his wiry locks, the young man had an unsettling resemblance to Frank's money-changer, the fellow he had talked to under the tree while they played dominos. These were the kind of fresh guys, Usnavy immediately thought to himself, who he worried would come near his daughter. He recognized them as the sort who would try to cop a feel on a crowded bus and laugh if anybody yelled at them to stop.

Finally, the clerk came back up, puffing on his cigarette, unhappy. Usnavy noticed there was a smattering of acne on his cheeks, like little scabbed pinpricks.

"What do you think?" Usnavy asked nervously. "Can it be fixed?"

The young man clicked his tongue, ignored him again, then screwed in a lightbulb and plugged the worn cord into the wall. After several tries, nothing happened.

"It's a piece of junk," the clerk declared with unrestrained disdain, stepping away from the desk, his bloated arms across his chest as if the lamp—and Usnavy—might contaminate him with a common virus.

"You mean the electricity . . ."

"Of course the electricity!" The clerk rolled his eyes and sighed heavily. The ashes at the tip of his cigarette floated away.

"But it's so beautiful . . ." Usnavy said, reaching to touch the rainbow-colored shade. There was one tiny marine panel in particular, he'd noticed, that seemed to ripple, as if there were water inside it.

"Beautiful?" the young man exclaimed. He slapped his free hand down on the desk in exasperation—startling Usnavy—then ground the cigarette into a dirty metal tray with the other.

Usnavy noted that they were very big hands, like baseball mitts, with thick, meaty fingers. Clearly, this boy did not labor on lamps or in any craft that required the slightest precision. In the jungle, he would have broken wood, maybe carried prey—sumptuous deer, antelope—but never killed, never carved. His was a brute strength, a matter of bulk rather than skill. This boy could pillage, this boy could break bones without a thought to the meaning of marrow.

"It's irreparably damaged, and it's not anything special—why would anybody want this lamp?" he asked scornfully.

Usnavy couldn't answer at first so he shrugged. "You're right, you're right," he said.

But when Usnavy went to take the lamp in his arms, the clerk didn't move; instead his eyes scanned it with his own nervous twitching.

"I'm . . . I'm sorry to have bothered you, compañero," Usnavy added.

The young man said nothing, just continued to stare as Usnavy reached around, winding the ragged cord about the base, embracing the lamp. In that acute spotlight, what should have been a simple chore became eternal and deliberate.

"Listen . . ." the clerk said at last, his voice lowered in a conspiratorial tone. "What do you really want, huh, old man?"

"What do I . . . ?" It was now Usnavy's turn to be disbelieving.

"I mean . . ." The clerk glanced around the office, even though there was nobody else there; the hard, round biceps under the Polo shirt would have been enough to scare anybody. Usnavy wondered immediately if the guy didn't have relatives in Miami sending him steroids, if his veins weren't filled with chemicals that might, if badly administered, cause him to erupt. "Why are you so obsessed with the lamp?"

"I'm not obsessed," Usnavy said stiffly. He'd heard that word before, many times, but always about the lamp in his room, the magnificent one, or the Revolution. For anyone to use it now to describe whatever he felt for this lesser creature seemed an insult to him. "I resent the insinuation," he added.

The young man straightened up, a hint of a smile on his lips. "All right," he said. "I'll tell you what . . . To help you out . . . I'll give you five dollars for it."

Five dollars! What he could do with five dollars—he could buy meat at the farmer's market, he could buy real soap! Usnavy's heart almost popped from his chest.

Five dollars! That was about 600 pesos!

Or, he thought in a flash, he could save it and try to scrape up another ten or fifteen dollars and get a bicycle for Nena. Where he'd get the rest of the money was not an issue then, so enthralled was he by the mere thought of having dollars.

This time, he promised himself and all the powers in the universe, the bike would be Nena's—he could walk; it was okay. If he somehow got that money for a bike for her, he could easily walk!

Desire was a new emotion for Usnavy: He had rarely coveted anything in his life. Even when he and Lidia made love, it was less a matter of yearning than an expression of gratitude, an antidote to loneliness. What was special with her was the selflessness, the security. They didn't talk about whether it was good—they didn't talk much at all—but rather purred or hiccupped, like cats or pigeons at the plaza.

But now, suddenly, Obdulio's presence in Usnavy's life had been replaced by an inexplicable craving. He could admit it now: He wanted a bike for Nena, he wanted a radio or TV for Lidia—maybe Obdulio was right and he could wish for a bigger place to live. He was not a Christian, he reminded himself: He could wish freely. Wasn't the Revolution about working for a better life for everyone—including himself? Didn't he, after all that time and effort, deserve a little something too? Wasn't it time for tomorrow to finally arrive?

Usnavy was so caught up with his own thoughts and rationalizations that he did not notice when another man entered the desolate lamp factory office. He was about Usnavy's age, but much worse for the wear: He walked with a serious limp, his hair was thinning, and he had a flat nose shaped like an upside down T, not the result of genetics but of a successful punch to the pug years ago. He was decked in overalls that suggested he worked with his hands—that he might perhaps even be employed by the factory assembling parts or whole fixtures—but there was something odd about him, strange little twinklings all over his chest and arms, as if he'd been dusted with a crushed star.

"Yoandry," the sparkly man said gruffly to the muscle boy at the desk. "Any luck? Did you get it?"

"No, no, but I'm trying," the clerk said, abruptly disregarding Usnavy and deferential, almost affectionate, toward the other client. "And how are you today, my friend?"

The sparkly man puffed up his cheeks and sighed in an exaggerated fashion. "I'm not having any luck finding anything at all!" he declared.

"What . . . what is it you're looking for?" Usnavy asked shyly.

"This American glass . . . Armstrong, stock number 2401, kind of chestnut brown on one side with very light white streaks on the other," the sparkly man said. Usnavy noticed even his face seemed to glitter. "Got it once, can't seem to find it again."

"Ah," Usnavy said uselessly. He had no idea what the guy was talking about.

"They're sheets of glass," the sparkly man said, taking in Usnavy's bewilderment. "I'd prefer the darker reddish-brown part, if I could find it. When back-lit, it's got a deep rust-brown color, with no red cast." Suddenly, he noticed the lamp in Usnavy's arms. "Hmm . . . a Tiffany?" he asked.

"No, no," Usnavy demurred, almost embarrassed. "I don't know what it is, really."

"Let me see," the man said, reaching for the base.

This must be where lamps reveal themselves, thought Usnavy, though nothing he'd read at the library had mentioned that. He noticed Yoandry, the clerk, was now shaking his leg impatiently. The fluorescent tube above them seemed to flicker in time with his anxiety, creating a mild strobe affect.

"Very splendid work," said the sparkly man, a pair of reading glasses now barely gripping his flat nose.

As the lamp was being probed, Usnavy felt the same way he did at the doctor's office when he went in for even the most routine examination: slightly abashed, a little panicky that they might find something that could have been avoided if only he'd known better.

"Is the lamp yours?" asked the sparkly man as he slipped off his reading glasses.

"Well, yes, sort of—I found it," Usnavy admitted, his head bowed.

"Lucky find."

"Lucky . . . what do you mean?" Hadn't the brawny boy said minutes ago that it was trash? In that moment of examination—while the sparkly man held the lamp upside down like a newborn—had his fortune turned?

"Well, it's a Tiffany, just like I thought, an original. See here? That's the Tiffany seal." He pointed to a T engraved at the base, with what looked like a couple of Ds and Cs clinging to it. "Sometimes Tiffany just signed *LTC*. There are a few paperweights—they're really medallions he gave to friends—which have his whole signature etched on the back. Not that he signed them, mind you. It was signed by a worker, of course. But it doesn't matter. Those—those are worth a mint."

"Really?" Usnavy asked, amazed.

So there was a Mr. Tiffany, a person; he'd had no idea. Tiffany to him was a style or, like Coca-Cola, a trademark. The few people who had seen his lamp—the magnificent one—always asked him if it was a Tiffany but he had never really known what to say. Now, having seen the signature, he would check the lamp as soon as he got home! (And, he quickly reminded himself, when he won Badagry's confidence, he would check her lamp too.)

But this other lamp, the little one, the one he'd rescued, the injured one—there was no dispute here. This was a real Tiffany—not a priceless medallion but a Tiffany nonetheless.

Realizing this, Usnavy's head snapped toward Yoandry, the liar. He should have called him out right then, should have at least made him fidget and worry, but instead it was Yoandry who was glaring darkly at Usnavy, the threat of harm clear in the two fat fists he'd laid on the desk for the old man to appreciate. This caused Usnavy to quake slightly.

"It's in terrible shape but I could fix it," said the sparkly man.

"Really?" Usnavy responded, realizing he was repeating himself in his nervousness, that he was very likely coming off like an idiot now.

"Yes, I could fix it. I mean, that's what I do—I work for the Fondo de Bienes Culturales; I fix lamps . . . Are you all right, compañero?"

"Yes, yes, quite. But the cost—"

"Yes, that's the thing. I could fix it, but I don't think you could afford it. See, it needs everything, really, although the base . . . hmm . . ." The sparkly man started contemplating the lamp again. "Nah, it'll cost too much."

Usnavy wanted to tell him that, in this case, he'd sell it for any price; he wanted to explain how, only minutes before, he had been pleased with the clerk's five-dollar offer—if he wanted to, the guy could fix it himself and sell it at a profit later, it didn't matter.

But the sparkly man didn't say a word about buying it and Yoandry, now sitting down and sporting a pout, was rolling his fists like cannon balls on the desktop.

"If you got it fixed, it could be worth a nice little penny for you," the artisan said. "But the cost . . ."

"Yeah, probably not worth it—it's not like this is a special or lost Tiffany or anything," said a smug Yoandry. Had he just winked conspiratorially at the sparkly man? Usnavy couldn't tell.

"A lost Tiffany?" he asked, confused.

"There are lots of uneditioned pieces," said the older man. "Some are real, some are fakes. A lot have been lost; no one knows where they are. So sometimes they're worth more, in a way, because of the mystique. But yours isn't one of those; yours has a number and everything."

"How do you know about all this stuff?" asked a leery Usnavy.

"My god!" exclaimed Yoandry from behind the counter, his meaty hands flying airless, propelled by the force of the insult embedded in Usnavy's question.

"It's okay, it's okay, compañero," the sparkly man said, gently patting the disconcerted boy's shoulder.

"See? What have I told you about the level of ignorance of the people who come in this place, huh?" the boy pleaded, his eyes shiny.

"Well, I apologize," Usnavy said, collecting his Tiffany from the counter, but he was sharply sarcastic, as offended as the clerk. "How will anyone ever learn without asking questions?"

"He's absolutely right!" agreed the sparkly man.

"Questions about lamps—yes!" the clerk implored. "But questions about your knowledge? How can you bear such stupid, disrespectful questions about your knowledge?"

This was too much drama for Usnavy, who was now clutching the injured lamp to his chest.

"Let me explain, compañero, let me explain," said the sparkly man, sitting Usnavy and his lamp down in a dirty plastic chair the lamp factory offered its potential customers.

Usnavy looked up at the flickering tube of light. He really needed to get to the bodega. People were waiting for him, people depended on him. But what choice did he have in any of this? Usnavy surrendered, his face in and out of the gentle strobe.

The way the sparkly man told it, Louis Comfort Tiffany didn't set out to make lamps; they were more of an accident. "He had this biography of himself commissioned at about the time his lamps were most popular and he only had them mentioned a couple of times. They couldn't be ignored—but how he wanted to ignore them!"

Usnavy rested his hands on the injured lamp. He could tell this could be awhile—this could, in fact, take longer than Frank and the guys' storytelling during the domino games. Why couldn't Mr. Tiffany be satisfied with the success of his lamps? If Mr. Tiffany had embraced his fate, Usnavy thought, he'd be free to walk away now, spared . . .

His mind wandered back to the sea, to Obdulio and his family. Had they made it? Where were they? Surely someone at the domino game would know by now about the end of that story.

But the sparkly man continued with his own narrative: Tiffany's father was a jeweler but the son was enamored of stained-glass murals. He eventually created a few, including a massive mosaic in Philadelphia, an extraordinary glass theatrical curtain in Mexico City.

"In fact, Tiffany didn't come up with the idea of the lamps at all," said the sparkly man, looking over at Yoandry for confirmation.

The boy had obviously heard the story many times. "That's right," he said, nodding vigorously. He could have been in the congregation of some visiting evangelist preacher from Harlem or Atlanta, shouting amens.

Amazingly enough, the sparkly man claimed the stained-glass lamps were actually his own grandfather's idea. "He worked for Tiffany as a gaffer, a glass blower," he explained, gesturing as if he were exhaling into a long pipe. "And one day, bored, he took some of the discarded glass from other projects and he made a lamp with an exceptional shade. Electricity was coming into vogue then, it was a big deal. The shades had to be different than before, with the old oil lamps. They had to be opaque. People say it was Thomas Edison who gave Tiffany the idea for the lamps, but it wasn't, it was my grandfather. And then Tiffany stole the idea."

"So your grandfather was American?" Usnavy asked, not paying strict attention, distracted by his own concerns, remembering the on-going exodus in Cojímar and wondering then why the sparkly man was still in Cuba. With an American relative, he could probably claim U.S. citizenship. Even if there were still people like Mayito, who could resist his wife's entreaties from the U.S., what some people wouldn't give for that!

"American? No, no—he was an immigrant to New York, an Italian glass blower from Murano who was hauled in to save Tiffany's fortunes when things got rough," the man said with a laugh.

"And a Jew," added Yoandry, rubbing his fingers together as if bill after bill were going through them.

The sparkly man chuckled. "This is important only because—I don't know if you know—glass blowing is an old Jewish art."

"I didn't know," said Usnavy, uneasy. He was now feeling totally trapped by the sparkly man and Yoandry, a reluctant audience to their story—a show he sensed he was not fully understanding, or perhaps worse, wasn't meant to understand. "So you're Jewish . . . Italian then . . . ?"

"I'm Cuban," the sparkly man said with a thump to his chest. "My grandfather and his entire immigrant crafts guild came to Cuba when Tiffany was hired to do the interior design for the Presidential Palace in the 1920s. I was born here, right here in Havana."

"You mean Mr. Tiffany worked on the Museum of the Revolution?" Usnavy asked, appalled. "But there's no stained-glass there."

The sparkly man and the clerk looked at each other for a suspended second then burst into laughter.

"Not now there isn't!" exclaimed Yoandry, his face wide and red from the hilarity.

Usnavy stood up; he'd had enough.

"Don't be offended, compañero, we're just laughing at life's absurdities, not at you," the sparkly man said and gently touched Usnavy's elbow. "Forgive us, we lost our manners. I wanted you to understand why I know a little about lamps. You see, it's in my blood."

Usnavy noticed the guy's hands were long and tapered, his nails shiny and healthy, the fingertips full of razor-thin scars. His fingerprints—the map of his hand—must change all the time, thought Usnavy.

That evening, Usnavy was late for his domino game. First, he had to rush to the bodega to store the injured lamp. There was no room in the tenement on Tejadillo, and besides, he didn't want to tell Lidia and Nena that he'd gotten it by rummaging in the trash, like their awful neighbors; he didn't want to relive that terrible moment when he'd told them the bike was stolen because of his carelessness and he'd caught the two of them looking at each other knowingly, worriedly.

At the bodega, his coworkers looked at him and the lamp askance and asked if he was all right. Conscience-stricken, Usnavy just muttered and lowered his eyes and hurried out again. He raced home for a dinner of salty white rice under the lustrous light of the magnificent one (the signature—damn it, he'd look for it later, when he had time) before making his way over to the comfort of the game and his friends.

"How I wish I had my bike," he complained under his breath as he moved along. The blister on his foot was growing, now a bubble of delicate skin that grazed the shoe's leather and caused him to wince with each step.

Even under normal circumstances, when it came to walking, Usnavy was not a typical Cuban. Most Cubans loved to stroll, to saunter about as if an actual destination were a second thought. But he hated walking, hated getting lost in the crowds, hated the way the air hung on him, sticky and hot. On foot everything took longer, especially now that the government was allowing artists and craftspeople to gather in certain parks in Old Havana and on the Malecón. People spilled onto the streets without regard, treating the sidewalks as storefronts or vitrines, showcasing their meager fruits, cheap watches, and spare parts (the rusted pedal from a sewing machine, for example, or the handle from a meat grinder). With the heat and humidity gripping him, Usnavy considered every gesture an exhausting struggle, as if he were living in slow motion.

"Guapón!" Frank yelled, pointing at his watch.

Usnavy was out of breath. He'd had to fight the crowds milling at the bus stops, as well as a bread line at a nearby shop, plus all the usual hustlers. The blister, he knew without looking, had burst; his skin was raw down there.

On his bike he could have avoided all of this. Since cars had practically disappeared because of the lack of fuel, on a bike the streets were now like thoroughfares. How he missed cruising downhill on his Flying Pigeon—how he yearned to glide on the open roads, the wind in his hair. (He never thought about driving a car, never imagined himself free behind the wheel, never longed for it at all.)

"What's the matter with you? This, now that we need you?" Frank said in mock reprimand. Frank loved to jab, loved to poke; most of the time, he didn't mean to hurt anybody, but sometimes he plain relished making people squirm, whether from pain or embarrassment; it was as if he couldn't tell the difference.

Usnavy threw himself down at the domino table, gasping like he never did when he rode. Why did his lungs prefer one mode so clearly over the other? Under the table, he discreetly pulled his foot out of his shoe, resting it on top, letting the burst blister breathe.

Without Obdulio, there were just four of them now, the exact number required to play. Sure, they could have had anybody else join in—in fact, it was perfectly common for neighbors to drop by the game to watch or ask in, and when one of the friends wanted a break, they'd let somebody else play (usually Oscar Luis, a former geologist turned cab driver who lived nearby). But by having the fifth man be one of their own—Usnavy—the friends had always kept complete control of the game. If somebody they didn't like showed up, they stalled. An extra man could make the wait last forever. Conversely, an extra man could pressure a stranger out of the game faster, if he got in at all.

The guys who watched regularly—the sapos, as they were affectionately called—all knew the rules, nobody had to tell them, and part of the entertainment value of the game resided precisely in how the friends dealt with strangers who showed up unexpectedly. That was grist for the best stories to tell later, at home to the wife or lover, at work the next day, or even later, right there on Montserrate, when the looming stars allowed the tale to go however it needed.

Yoandry, the sparkly man, and their Tiffany tales had nothing on these guys, thought Usnavy, who loved going home and regaling Lidia with accounts harvested at the domino games.

"All right, you and Mayito," Frank ordered Usnavy. They were each, in their own way, dealing with Obdulio's absence. In Frank it manifested in a gruffer than usual style, his eyes floating, averting contact with everybody.

"Ah, c'mon, give me a break," Mayito protested, speaking unexpectedly. "No offense, Usnavy, you're my brother but you're salao, man. These days you lose every single time. The thing with the doubles the other day—that was the topper."

"I'm not salao," Usnavy said, "not anymore." How could he explain? It would be easier to decipher the mystery of the rock-hewn churches at Lalibela, where angels were said to have worked side by side with African artisans.

"What do you mean *not anymore?*" asked Frank, leaning back, a grin erupting on his big rubbery Anthony Quinn face.

"I mean . . . Look, I just know I'm not salao anymore, okay?" No one would understand—especially these guys, who believed in nothing. But in his soul Usnavy knew that, in spite of everything, that broken lamp would bring him luck. It had to. It had hit him on the way home from Lámparas Cubanas: Now that Obdulio had left, things were so horrible, there was no other way to go. It was a matter of time.

"Okay," Frank replied, "whatever you say, guapo." He winked at Diosdado, who ignored him. "Let's try out your new luck."

Just then a group of foreign tourists sidled up to the game, smiling and nodding. The sapos stepped back with a sudden meekness, parting so that the tourists had a ringside view. Frank reclined and smirked, his cigar held extravagantly between his teeth. One of the foreign women ran up and posed, her flushed face above his shoulders while Frank leaned back, macho and sure, and another tourist took a picture, its unnecessary flash blinding everyone. Mayito squinted and rubbed his eyes. Usnavy thought he was going to be sick, the flickering light stirring the acids in his nearly empty belly.

A second woman—quite possibly the guide—then put her hands on Diosdado's shoulders (an unexpected, disturbing familiarity), prepping to model for the photographer.

But, to everyone's surprise, Diosdado shook her off. "No," he said firmly, looking at her over his bifocals, his eyes like simmering coal. "No," he said again, but the tourists argued with him in English.

Frank tried to negotiate. "C'mon, what can it hurt?" he said to his friend, shrugging.

But Diosdado remained firm: "No, I said no."

"But why not?" Frank pushed. "You afraid of 'em, is that it? Are you an Indian or something and think they're going to steal your image, or what?"

"Frank, leave him alone," muttered Mayito.

"Why do I have to explain myself?" Diosdado demanded.

All the while, the tourists pressed, snapping away at the dominos on the table, at Frank acting tough, at the guys from the neighborhood, with their ragged pride and awkward postures. Finally, one of the tourists defiantly focused his lens on Diosdado and teased with the possibility of shooting him against his will.

Diosdado again raised his eyes above the rim of his glasses. "You guys are just going to go along with this, aren't you?" he said to the sapos. "Why? Because they're foreigners? So what?"

Usnavy laughed but he was on Diosdado's side. He remembered the American missionary and his Cuban converts down by the cathedral and, without thinking at all, started to clap, first slowly, then more feverishly. And then the sapos—the autistic kid the loudest of all—followed, their rhythm full of spite, pushing the tourists away from the table, crowding them out until the only camera shot they would have had was of the Cubans' backs.

Frank, however, did not clap. Long after the tourists walked away, he sat there darkly, his eyes fixed on Diosdado. As Mayito noisily stirred the dominoes to begin the game, Usnavy realized Frank wasn't going to let the incident go. In the meantime, Diosdado leaned back from the table, his broad brow furrowed, unusually intense behind his blurry bifocals. It seemed to Usnavy that Frank and Diosdado had always been going at it.

"Anybody hear from Obdulio?" Frank asked, his cigar going up and down in his mouth. The way he asked indicated to Usnavy that the question was rhetorical, that somehow Frank had already managed to find out—in just a few days—how it was going for Obdulio in his new life in Miami. Diosdado squirmed in his seat.

"He made it, no? I mean, that's what I heard at the bodega," said Usnavy, too eagerly, then saw right away that he had inadvertently played into the set-up. Initially, he had been relieved to hear that Obdulio had arrived safely but then he had gotten all tangled up: He really wanted to wish him well though he was sad, hurt, flustered, maybe—to his horror—even a little jealous that, suddenly, Obdulio no longer shared the same worries. No doubt Obdulio wouldn't be worried about what his family would have to eat.

"Yeah, all the way to Key West—no problem at all," said Frank as he selected his dominos one by one from the scrambled pieces. "Got picked up at the beach by his brother, like he'd been on a fishing trip or something ordinary like that."

The sapos gave each other quick, knowing looks. Usnavy wondered how many of them were calculating their own odds against the currents of those ninety miles, how many would be up on that rocky beach in Cojímar that very night, testing their buoyancy and courage. Thousands of Cubans like them had already made their way to the Florida shores that summer, joined by almost as many Haitians fleeing their own island—in Usnavy's mind, a place of real nightmares, a wasteland of wanton violence and rampant disease. (He could understand why those people left Haiti, that made sense to him.)

In recent days, there had been reports that the U.S. was planning to invade Haiti and Usnavy, wary of how expansive the assault might be, had allowed himself at scattered moments to fret about whether they were safe in Cuba, and what might happen if the Americans changed course and dropped on their coasts instead. With so many people leaving, everything was already so uncertain. Who would be left to put up a defense?

"Felicidades, Obdulio, mi hermano," a teenage boy called out to their exiled friend as if Obdulio were across the street, down the block, or passing by on a bicycle. "Remember us, don't forget us—send us something!" He formed his hands into a prayer and laughed, immediately joined by the others in his desire and resignation. Usnavy knew they were dreaming of Belgian chocolates and Schick razors, Motorola radios and Michael Jordan.

Almost instantly, Usnavy wondered how many of these guys had been involved in those unseemly riots earlier in the month, when hundreds of people had started yelling and fighting with the police on the Malecón. After the first flush of rage, some of the protesters had smashed cars and store windows, looting like rioters in American cities. Usnavy had been appalled. The rabble had been shouting epithets at El Comandante—"Down with the tyranny!"—until The Man himself showed up, stern and strong, and then the chant changed abruptly to vivas and hurrahs.

"I know Obdulio was going to check in with Reynaldo once he got there," said Frank. "Diosdado, you heard anything from your son?"

Usnavy decided to keep as quiet as possible. He could tell Frank was circling Diosdado, intoxicating himself with the very idea of his prey.

"No," Diosdado said sharply. "Who starts?" he asked, adjusting his bifocals and staring at his pieces as if each little dot made up a larger picture, like a constellation in the sky, Orion or Pegasus. It was Usnavy and Mayito against the tense partnership between Diosdado and Frank.

"Did Obdulio have Reynaldo's phone number?" Frank dogged on. "You gave it to him, didn't you? I know he was going to ask you for it." He scrunched up his nose, as if the smell of the blood was already too strong, an ache almost.

"Are we playing or what?" Diosdado demanded, eyeing Frank over the rim of his glasses. The sapos stiffened at Diosdado's frosty rejoinder. On the bottom half of his bifocals, his pores looked like moon craters.

"We're playing," Frank said, throwing down a double nine like a dare. He had a huge, malleable grin on his face.

Mayito quickly followed with a nine-eight and Diosdado tapped the other end with a nine-two. Usnavy dropped a double eight. Mayito's eyebrows arched instantly.

"Man, I thought you said your luck had changed—you're not packed with doubles again, are you? Because if you are, we're stopping the game right now, got it?" Frank demanded of Usnavy.

The sapos giggled. Usnavy did too. He actually had a pretty good hand. Frank threw down his piece, followed immediately by Mayito. Then Diosdado made his play, an eight-two on Usnavy's double, without a word.

"No commentary tonight, guapo?" Frank asked.

"I'm tired," Usnavy said. "I've been running around all day."

The spectators muttered among themselves but Usnavy couldn't tell if it was curiosity or disappointment. He could hear the sloshing of upturned rum bottles, the gurgling of sloppy drinking even this early in the evening.

"Oh yeah? Tired from what?" Frank asked as he played.

"Errands, just errands," Usnavy said.

It wasn't that he didn't trust his friends with knowledge of the injured lamp and Mr. Tiffany. But their whole lives, they'd been the ones with the street smarts, not him. He wanted, for once, to do something that might surprise them, something that could actually earn him respect instead of just affection. Besides, he was still unsure about what he was doing, exactly.

Somebody handed him a thimble full of coffee and he downed it without thinking. It was strong and black and delicious.

Mayito placed a piece on the table and Usnavy, glad to be able to play something other than a double, smiled broadly as he took his turn. The coffee's taste lingered on his tongue and throat.

"Hey, maybe you're not salao after all," said Frank, leaning back, getting into position. The smile expanded even more, stretched until all his other features seemed to disappear behind it. "In fact, when you really think about it, guapo, maybe you were never salao at all. You got all the wonders and benefits of our socialist system, to which you subscribe like the Apostles to Jesus—except, of course, for the traitorous Judas, and maybe Peter too, because you have to wonder, don't you, if the way he passed down Christ's teachings was the way Jesus would have liked . . . I mean, with the church such an avaricious and oppressive institution . . ."

There were uh-huhs but also grumblings behind him from the audience, many of whom sported around their necks crucifixes or medallions with saints (right alongside brightly beaded necklaces that connoted other, contradictory beliefs). Their grumblings were less fervor than habit, but in either case Frank's words were unsettling, like silent lightning before the shattering of thunder.

When it was his turn, Diosdado dropped his piece without even looking up.

"But that aside, yes, you're lucky—you have a wife who loves you and would never cheat," Frank continued with a fake felicity, "a daughter you can count on to be your daughter forever. Because Nenita is a real girl, after all, a real girl—"

"What do you mean?" Usnavy sat up straight. "Of course she's a real girl . . ."

Frank played without hesitation, smacking each piece down with a broad, dramatic arching of his arms. "That's what I'm saying—you can go to sleep knowing Nena's a real girl and get up the next day knowing Nena's a real girl—that's a kind of security in this crazy world, no?"

Mayito, disgusted, clicked his tongue as he pushed in his piece. "Frank . . ." he said softly.

The sapos started making faces at each other, not sure where Frank was going. (Frank produced enough good stories; he was worth the wait.)

"My god, yes, she's a real girl! What are you saying, that she's not Pinocchio?" Usnavy exclaimed. It seemed like a ridiculously obvious thing. "But that's not luck—that's natural!" The sapos giggled at Usnavy's assertion.

"That's what I'm saying! That's it exactly! But in this world you can't take that for granted, can you? What do you think, Diosdado?" Frank said, widening his eyes in mock innocence.

The sapos were startled: What was Frank getting at? They stared while Diosdado inspected his pieces as if in deep concentration, but Usnavy noticed a slight tremor in his hand. "Are you going to play, Usnavy, or are you going to continue with this ludicrous discussion?" Diosdado asked icily.

Was it his turn already? "Yes, yes, of course I'm playing," Usnavy said, giving his pieces a quick glance. His stomach took a little bounce too.

"You didn't say what you think, muchachón," Frank dared Diosdado.

The sapos leaned closer. Usnavy could feel the heat of their bodies and smell the ever-present rum, like gasoline spilled around kindling. He slid his blistered foot back in his shoe, just in case.

Diosdado refused to lift his eyes from the slats in his hands. "What I think about what?" he asked.

"You know . . ."

The smile, Frank's smile; it was a trap, Usnavy could see it coming down on his poor pal Diosdado and there was nothing anyone could do, not even Mayito, who was now staring at his dominos in utter revulsion. The murmurs from the sapos were creating a curtain of noise, like radio static, behind them.

"No, I don't know," Diosdado finally said, folding over his pieces with a hard slap that made both Usnavy and Mayito jump. Their own dominos wobbled then fell over haphazardly, exposing about half of them. The crowd hushed. Miraculously, Frank's pieces stayed up.

"Yes, you do; you know exactly what I'm talking about," Frank said, chewing his cigar ever more furiously, making it go up and down like a piston. He leaned up on the table and covered his pieces with his hands, laying them down without making a sound. "About Reynaldo . . . or should I say *Reina* . . . ?"

A red-faced Diosdado shot out of his seat, taking the table with him and hurling the black and yellow dominos all over the street. Mayito lost his balance and almost fell backward while the sapos erupted in protests at Frank for goading Diosdado and at Diosdado for not being able to take it. Rum spilled, some even splashing onto Usnavy, who quickly tried to wipe it off, not wanting to show up at home later and have Lidia worry more than she already did.

Frank cackled wickedly. The autistic boy, expressionless and unmoved by the commotion, got up from his chair and stood expressionless, then began to pick up the dominos.

"Fuck, man, whatever it is, it's not that big a deal," said Jacinto, the neighbor from Tejadillo who'd sewn Usnavy's shoe together. He called after Diosdado, but he was already a block away, his stubby legs hurrying from the scene.

"I hate this," muttered Mayito as he scrambled to his feet.

"Be cool, man," Chachi said to everyone and no one in particular. He was married to Yamilet, Usnavy's neighbor.

"That was unnecessary," Mayito said directly to Frank as he bent over to help pick up the scattered dominos.

Frank straightened his shirt, tucked it into his pants, and pumped his chest out like a shield. "That's what he gets for raising a faggot," he said in his own defense.

The sapos jerked to attention; Jacinto winced.

Usnavy shook his head. That was news? "C'mon, Frank, we've all known about Reynaldo since he was—what?—twelve? Why harass Diosdado now, for god's sake?"

"Because," said Frank with an unusually serious timbre, "Reynaldo is not Reynaldo anymore: He's really Reina."

"Cómo?" asked a skeptical Oscar Luis from the crowd.

"So?" asked Usnavy with a shrug. He was, admittedly, confused, but he didn't really care what Reynaldo was doing with his life. It had nothing to do with him, or them, and he was so far away now.

"So, you dimwit—that little faggot had his wee-wee cut off. He had that operation. He's Reina now. Legally. The motherfucker is a woman now!" Frank explained; he seemed to be marching in place as he talked, so proud was he of being able to deliver this information.

"Coño!" Jacinto exclaimed.

The sapos oooh-ed and aaah-ed, everybody suddenly covering, touching, or grabbing their own parts, imagining the agony of having them sliced away, their laughter a transparent defense.

Mayito nodded, not approvingly, but to affirm the facts of the story. "None of our business, though, none of our business," he continued under his breath, his Buddha face sagging.

Almost immediately, Chachi started joking. "So did he get big ones, huh?" he asked, using his hands to shape two global spheres on his chest. The sapos yelped with glee.

"And what about back here?" Oscar Luis giggled, grabbing his own ass.

But Usnavy couldn't fathom any of it. "How do you know about any of this, huh?" he asked Frank.

"How do I know? Because Obdulio arrives in Miami delighted to call Reynaldo, and who shows up but Reina!"

"Maybe it was a joke," Usnavy suggested. "Maybe Obdulio got confused, huh, did you think about that? He just got there; he might not know how things are yet."

Around him, the guys chuckled, shaking their heads. Was it at Reynaldo (or Reina), or at Obdulio, or at him? Usnavy pulled at his T-shirt, soaked from careless rum, and held it away from his skin.

Frank continued: "No, man, it's true: Reynaldo's a woman now. But you know what bothers me? You know what it is?" He poked Usnavy in the chest with his finger, right on the wet spot. "Diosdado knew—he's known for years. And that jerk never told us. Never."

Around them people nodded and shuffled. Mayito stepped away from the circle, shaking his head. "Why would he?" he grumbled, but he wasn't talking to anybody in particular anymore.

"Imagine that!" Jacinto exclaimed.

The sapos, laughing and joking among themselves, were dispersing now. Whether they understood Frank's gripe enough to process it didn't matter. Each would take the story, chew it up good, then practice how they would tell it later, adding little bits and pieces to their individual versions, each according to his need.

That night when he got home, Usnavy found his worried wife out in the courtyard on Tejadillo, pacing among the tenement's gossips and hustlers. It had taken him awhile longer than usual to arrive, not because he was walking instead of riding now, but because, first, he'd strolled over to the Malecón to replay the clapping that had scared off the tourists, to think through what he'd found out about Diosdado and Reynaldo, and then what Frank had done.

At the Malecón, he'd seen young girls Nena's age strut as if on a runway for the benefit of the foreign men who drove by in rented cars. The girls were brazen: As if dipped in Lycra, their clothes accented every crevice of their young bodies, every slope and incline of their new breasts. They yelled out "Spain!" or "Italy!" to the cars, all loaded with men Usnavy's age who looked as if they couldn't believe they'd stumbled onto this paradise, their expressions of joy so exaggerated that even the most benign grandfather among them seemed maniacal.

As he neared the water, Usnavy had found himself particularly struck by the full figure strolling in front of him, flabby hips swinging wildly, almost like a bell. He thought he could hear it striking, a loud and forceful tone that paralyzed him. But when the womanly shape turned, she startled Usnavy—wasn't there something a bit off in her face? Wasn't her nose too bulbous, her mouth too cavernous and labrose, her laugh too robust?

At the water's edge, Usnavy had leaned forward and inhaled the sea, letting the spray cover him. The waves climbed and curled, then crashed among themselves. Maybe the salt would crystallize and he'd be like the sparkly man, giving off light wherever he went. It had been such a long day.

"Lidia, are you all right?" Usnavy asked when he saw his wife in the courtyard at Tejadillo, her house dress wrapped tightly around her timid body, her feet tucked sloppily into plastic sandals. "I'm sorry . . . I didn't mean to worry you. I went for a walk after the game. You won't believe what happened."

Lidia grabbed at his sleeve, not to reproach him but for refuge. "Usnavy . . ."

"What? What's going on?" he asked, taking her softly by the shoulders.

"It's Nena . . ."

"Nena!" He'd forgotten to go to the hospital to get her papers for the new ID! Nena was wandering Havana like an undocumented alien, like those desperate Haitians who tried to pass as Orientales but whose French and Creole accents always gave them away.

"Yes, the police . . ."

Usnavy thought his heart stopped for an instant. Whatever trouble she'd gotten into was no doubt his fault for being so irresponsible, so focused on other things beside his daughter. He shook his head in dismay.

"They brought her home," Lidia sputtered.

"What . . . ?" Usnavy asked, jerking back, suddenly out of breath.

"She's okay, she's fine," Lidia said, patting him on the chest. "But—"

"What happened?" he asked, pulling Lidia into the shadows between their water barrel and the door, away from the prying eyes of the neighbors that, Usnavy thought, all suddenly seemed as large and portentous as the feline pupils floating in their room. Rosita, the woman who made sandwiches from blankets, ambled by and winked at him knowingly. She was brazenly carrying a couple of pieces of cloth across her arm.

"Nena went to see the Campos family," Lidia explained while pushing back a lock of hair.

Usnavy had to think: *The Campos . . .*

"For god's sake, Usnavy—the Campos—the people who used to live down the street, who gave her that poster of the American singer when they moved to Miami!" a frustrated Lidia said, her eyes moist and red.

He couldn't remember the last time he'd seen her so upset. "Did they do something to her?"

"No, Usnavy, no—they didn't do anything. What happened was . . . when she went to see the Campos, she didn't have an ID to show—"

Usnavy flinched.

"Not that it would have mattered, since the police wouldn't have let her go up to their room at the Habana Libre anyway."

Usnavy slumped against the wall. There was no way around that. Even with an ID, Cubans needed to be on official business to enter hotels, everybody knew that. And there was never any business beyond the lobby considered official, if that.

"And . . . and Nena resisted," said Lidia, looking at the floor. "I don't know all the details, she hasn't told me and I don't even know where to begin. But she got in an argument with the police. They had to drag her out of there. When they brought her to our door, she wasn't any calmer."

Usnavy ran his hand over his face. Nena was an exemplary student who'd breezed through her initiation into the Union of Communist Youth. She did volunteer work with a Jamaican benevolent society that had a small chapter in Havana (this, though it was much harder to get people to admit to a Jamaican past in Havana than in Oriente). She had been elected to leadership posts at her school's camp in the countryside. How could this happen?

"We're failing her. We need to pay more attention to her, buy her things—I don't know!" exclaimed an exasperated Lidia.

"Buy her things? She has all she needs!" Usnavy protested.

"All she needs? Oh, Usnavy, don't you get it? She's a girl, a girl turning into a young woman. She needs things you can't even imagine."

"Well, if I can't even imagine then—"

"You know what I mean!"

"What do you want me to do, Lidia? Break the law? Steal? Would that make you and her both happy?" Obdulio's fading figure crossed his mind, his raft held together with the illicit rope. Usnavy felt his throat grow dry and tried to move his tongue around, to scare up some spit.

"What would make me happy is if you weren't so naïve . . . If we have all we need, why can't we try and get her something extra now and again? I don't know, a decent pair of shoes . . . *I don't know*! This is going to kill you?"

"Everything requires dollars! Where am I going to get dollars?" Of course, he'd been thinking about this already—about the injured lamp, about getting Nena her own bike, but he couldn't say anything yet. After all, he still hadn't figured out any kind of plan. He still didn't have a clue what to do. He still didn't have a single dollar to his name.

"I don't know, Usnavy, where does everybody else get dollars?"

"Okay, okay," he said. He had to figure something out.

"No, Usnavy, it's not okay," Lidia insisted. "Everybody saw what happened, how she . . ." Lidia's voice drifted off and she stamped her foot, crossing her arms across her waist as if she had a stomachache.

"How she what? How she what?" Usnavy demanded, desperate.

"My god, she was reciting Guillén at the top of her voice: *I have—*"

"Lidia, Lidia—I know how it goes!" Usnavy exclaimed in a fierce whisper.

Ever since he could remember, Nicolás Guillén's "Tengo," an early celebration of the Revolution, was required reading for every Cuban school child:

> *When I, just yesterday, look*
> *and recognize myself, me, Juan Nobody,*
> *and today Juan Somebody,*
> *I have everything today,*
> *I open my eyes, I see,*
> *I touch myself and see*
> *and ask myself how things have come to be this way.*
> *I have, let's see,*
> *the pleasure of strolling through my country,*
> *master of everything within it,*
> *with things at hand that*
> *I didn't or couldn't have before.*
> *I can say harvest,*
> *I can say mountains,*
> *I can say city,*
> *I can say army,*
> *forever mine and yours, ours,*
> *a vast array*
> *of light, star, flower.*
> *I have, let's see,*
> *the pleasure of going—*
> *me, a peasant, a worker, an ordinary person—*

I have the pleasure of going
(it's just an example)
to a bank to speak with the manager,
not in English,
not as sir or madam,
but as compañero, the way we talk in Spanish.
I have, let's see,
being a black man,
the right not to be stopped
at the door of a dancehall or bar,
or at the desk at some hotel,
and be screamed at because there aren't any rooms,
not even a small room, not a huge one,
a tiny room in which I can rest.
I have, let's see,
freedom from any rural guard
who might grab me and lock me in a cell,
who might seize me and toss me from my land
into the middle of the road.
I have, like the earth, the sea as well,
no country club,
no highlife,
no tennis and no yacht,
but shore upon shore and wave upon wave,
immense, blue, open, democratic:
indeed, the sea.
I have, let's see,
the fact that I have learned to read,
to count,

I have learned to write,
and reason
and laugh.
I have—I now have
where to work
and earn
what I need to eat.
I have, let's see,
I have what I should have had.

Usnavy thought: And now what? Now what was he going to do?

In their room, a tired Nena was already bundled under the bed sheet, the magnificent lamp lightless above her, leaving her parents to gaze at her blurry black figure on the mattress. A schoolbook lay open, face-down, next to her.

But on stepping into the room, Usnavy's sewed-up right shoe slid on a puddle of oily water, causing him to do an awkward dance right at the door, barking like a frightened pup, his arms flailing. Nena jerked on the bed. As Lidia steadied him, Usnavy got embarrassed at the spectacle he'd just made, and suddenly felt too ridiculous for the serious talk he was planning to have with his daughter.

"It's because of Chachi and Yamilet," Lidia whispered to him about the puddle, her pupils pointing up, past the lamp. "The ceiling's leaking."

Usnavy shook her off, annoyed. He turned on the light and picked up a paperback of Jesús Díaz's *Los Años Duros* from the wet floor, its cover buckling and bubbling, ruined. "I wish we'd had a son," he said, meaning to spite her and regretting it instantly. Because she'd grabbed him again, Usnavy felt the impact of his words immediately: Lidia's muscles turned taut, like blankets being wrung by powerful hands.

The comment had been exceptionally mean: Lidia had wanted a boy more than anything, more than he certainly, and had almost died in the long torturous process of bringing Nena into the world. She had confessed to Usnavy a strange mix of pride in her own twenty-two-hour endurance, but she'd also been transparently disappointed in the baby. While Usnavy had beamed at the two of them, all Lidia could say as Nena took to her breast, bewildered, was, "A girl . . ." Lidia had insisted that growing up female brought problems that were only magnified in hard times yet Usnavy didn't care: His baby girl was a gift, light in its purest form.

"I . . . I'm sorry," Usnavy said right away, his mind back to the day's revelation about Reynaldo. Oh god, he thought, be careful what you wish for—what if Nena heard him or sensed his whim, even if it was only fleeting and facile? What if his carelessness provoked some errant angel to take her away? That would be worse than anything, that would be worse than seeing her singing Christian songs or standing at the traffic lights at the Malecón, stopping strangers in cars.

He would have gone on thinking this way were it not for the fact that, to his amazement, Lidia pushed him away, hard, with both hands, refusing his apology and turning from him.

"Lidia . . ." he whispered to her.

She remained firm, her arm outstretched, as steady and implacable as his invisible giants. He leaned on her but she was unmoved.

"Lidia, please," he said, but she refused him again, taking to the bed with Nena, her back against her daughter's in perfect alignment, and now using her own legs to keep her husband from coming any closer.

Lying next to her, Nena—clearly awake now—stiffened. Her schoolbook toppled to the wet floor with a tiny splash.

"I didn't mean it, Lidia," Usnavy whispered, picking up the textbook
and trying to dry it off with his shirt. He glanced up at the magnificent
lamp and its blinding light, for a second distracted, scanning the brilliance for the telltale signature he'd recently learned about. "It's just . . .
it's been a horrible day, a horrible day."

"You're salao, Usnavy," his wife rasped with finality. "And because
of you, we're all salao too."

III.

The next day Usnavy woke up to a ruckus in the courtyard. In the black of his crowded room, he turned, covering his eyes with his forearm, pleading for more darkness, more sleep. The lamp overhead was numb, a vague cloud. He heard Nena and Lidia rustling under the bed sheet, rearranging their limbs. The air in the room was sour. Outside, there was yelling and fighting, but Usnavy couldn't quite tell over what. In the background, there was a flickering of something else: a kind of laugh, but he didn't recognize it right away. It was weightless and slick. It lacked the full-throated gaiety of his neighbors, the sardonic undertone of his friends. It was not a Cuban laugh.

Usnavy sat up, startled. He pulled on his pants and cracked open the door. The light outside was blinding, a white wash with only the slightest bits of color or form.

Everyone's faces appeared distorted, their mouths red ovals, eyes shaped in the same feline fashion as the magnificent lamp that remained unlit in his room.

Usnavy closed his own lids tight, imagining his neighbors' faces as Kwele Gon masks, their wearers anonymous and immune, using fear to their advantage and taking matters into their own hands: justly redistributing food, gasoline, even the space in the tenements, ending all of their troubles in one carnivalesque performance. *I believe, I believe,* intoned Usnavy, though he never got more precise than that these days.

But, of course, when he opened his eyes he was not in an idyllic Ginen, but here, where it was just another day in a traumatized Havana.

"What's going on?" Usnavy asked a boy standing outside his door, leaning on the water barrel. He thought he recognized the boy, a sapo from the domino games.

Usnavy could see to the center of the courtyard where a group of men were laughing. One of them, Jacinto, was holding his penis in his hand through the hole in his boxer shorts. He and another guy, a foreigner, were slapping each other around, giddy. By the casually faded wear of his jeans and elaborate but dirty sneakers, Usnavy pegged the tourist as American.

"Jacinto was trying to neutralize a curse his ex-wife put on him— you shoulda seen it, old man, that woman piled a dead chicken and this black powder and all kinds of brujería right at his door," the boy said breathlessly. "But Jacinto, he just comes out and pees all over it."

"Uh huh," Usnavy nodded as Jacinto tucked his member back in his shorts and extended his unhygienic right hand to the American, who was still so amused, or so drunk or high, that he thought nothing of shaking it.

Usnavy knew that Jacinto's mother would have been horrified by her son's behavior. But as Usnavy surveyed the crowd and didn't see her anywhere in sight, he remembered she'd been sick the last few months. She needed a certain vitamin, Jacinto had told him, which they couldn't find, even on the black market, something foreign-made and as elusive to them on the island as air to a drowning man. Since Jacinto had moved in with her after the nasty separation from his wife, he'd been doing little more than trying to take care of her.

"So then this yuma comes out from Yamilet's room and, you know, her husband Chachi, he sees Jacinto with his dick in his hand and he starts yelling at him, that he's gonna freak out the foreigner, that he's some kind of underdeveloped ape, but—get this—the American, he sees Jacinto peeing on the dead chicken and the black powder and stuff and, like, maybe he's still silly from whatever Yamilet did to him, right? Because he gets this big grin on his face, like this is the most amazing thing he's ever seen, and when Chachi notices that, he changes his tune and he's begging Jacinto to pee some more, cause the foreigner's into it. Of course, Jacinto holds back a little when he sees what's going on . . . he just stands there, shakes his dick a little, like to let Chachi know he's got more, but that if Chachi and Yamilet are getting some fula from that foreigner cause he's peeing over a dead chicken, then they'd better share. Then—and this is wild—the yuma just cracks up and starts clapping and slaps Jacinto on the shoulder and hands him a five-dollar bill and Jacinto sprays the whole damn courtyard!"

"Five dollars!" exclaimed Usnavy. "Five dollars for peeing in public?"

"Yeah," the boy said, "over a dead chicken!"

Everything's in flux, thought Usnavy: Yesterday the city was beautiful, the sea cradled the island in a warm embrace. But now the city was Nubia, Napata, Kush—there was water everywhere but in the pipes, in the plumbing where it should be a veritable river. Water in millions of muddy puddles on the streets, water bringing down whole buildings, water crashing malevolently all along the shores. There was water right under Usnavy's bare feet.

Stepping outside his door while pulling on his sewed-up shoe, Usnavy couldn't recognize Jacinto, the Angolan War hero, in that moment of forced folklore out in the courtyard. For months now he hadn't been able to figure out Chachi and Yamilet, both former teachers; everyone knew she jerked off the local cop to keep him off her back about everything she and her husband were doing.

The island's frustrated experiment and those ninety miles of endless water suddenly made all of them so desperate that Jacinto could pull a stunt like that, and an old man like Obdulio could forsake his whole life for the chance at something as banal as driving a car.

"I need some coffee," he muttered to no one in particular. "I need to sit down." The boy who had told him what was going on had vanished.

Usnavy walked through the tenement, leaving Lidia and Nena still in their bed, past the jovial neighbors, past the funnel of flies that was the bathroom, out to Tejadillo through the huge arch of the door he knew had once (long ago) belonged not to this slum but to a glorious mansion, a castle of a house where he would have never been welcome. As the day began in earnest, somebody somewhere in the tenement let loose an explosion of music, cymbals crashing and horns blaring from an imported stereo.

"Aaaaah . . ." Usnavy groaned, holding his head. He walked faster and faster, hurrying away, every joint jabbing with pain.

He was cursed, too, with remembering, with having fresh in his mind the pulverizing poverty of Caimanera and Guantánamo, of his mother's humiliations, of panhandling (though he'd never, ever, told anyone in Havana, not even Lidia) as a young boy outside the bars and brothels where the Yankee soldiers hung out, his gummy fingers outstretched, the coins heavy in his hands.

He was also cursed with remembering the exhilaration, the euphoria of 1959, and the struggles that he gladly signed onto with the idea that no Cuban boy would ever have to hold out his hand again, that no Cuban woman would ever have to sit still in a room with foreigners and laugh at their stupid jokes or pretend to find their boorish antics charming.

In his torment, Usnavy kept walking and walking, ignoring the invisible giants who stepped aside when he went by. As he rushed past the Malecón, a commotion drew his attention. This was now Casablanca, where illegal goods were bought and sold and legal ones bartered; men and women shivered in their dealings, then turned their eyes quickly away; they all ran as soon as the sale was concluded.

Every night, this is where the journeys begin, thought Usnavy, where the first steps are taken, where someday I'll be left alone, all alone, staring at those distant lights . . .

But as Usnavy went over to the crowd, the usually anxious vendors, buyers, and barely disguised balseros were all bent over the edge of the Malecón, peering at the water. Usnavy craned his neck, stretched it up like a periscope to see empty overalls, the kind the sparkly man had worn that day at Lámparas Cubanas, the bloody extremities shredded by spiny shark teeth, the beast now surely satisfied and humming somewhere in that dreadful sea as the remains floated up to shore.

That day, Usnavy was late for work. Of course, he hadn't gone his usual straight route, wandering instead. There, at an unfamiliar park, seniors were stretching and breathing Tai Chi. They held their weightless arms out from them, flightless cranes futilely aiming for the sky. He wasn't even thinking about work until he suddenly found himself so far from his neighborhood that he had to hurriedly grab a taxi back.

It was one of the unofficial ones—in fact, illegal (Lidia had scoffed at them once but he realized he no longer knew what she'd think)—the kind that sneaks up slowly on its customers while the driver whispers his services. Under normal circumstances, Usnavy wouldn't be a potential customer; wind-swept on his bike, he'd be spared the dilemma of having to even consider whether to ride or not.

But he was late; he could tell by the position of the sun in the hazy sky, by the harshness of the light. Reluctantly, he waved it down, climbed in, settled his spine and stretched his legs. The taxi was a big, roomy Chevy, lathered with sea-blue house paint on the outside, held together by duct tape and rope on the inside, its motor wheezing like an old lion. The air coming through the opened window blended with the fumes and smoke. It was not refreshing, it was not liberating.

"My bike," Usnavy moaned, but the driver, engulfed in his own thoughts, paid him no mind.

The few pesos to ride would have been a bit of a luxury for Usnavy, but since the cab ran out of gas and coughed to a stop before quite reaching Old Havana, he got away with giving the dismayed driver a couple of Cuban coins—and only because he felt kind of sorry for him. Who knew when and from where fuel would come?

He left the driver pounding on the hood just off the Museum of the Revolution, filled with display case after display case of bloody clothes and guns; the guards there turned their faces away from the scene with the dead cab. Back when the museum was the presidential palace and Mr. Tiffany and the sparkly man's grandfather were doing the interior decoration—chandeliers and marble busts of the hemisphere's heroes (including Abraham Lincoln and Benito Juárez), mahogany chests and ebony tables—who would have predicted revolution, who would have predicted any of this chaos now?

As Usnavy walked to the bodega, he couldn't help but notice all the new turistaxis lined up at the Seville Hotel, mostly Japanese makes, with their tinted windows hiding the drivers and the simpering foreigners inside, including whole new hordes of Spaniards and illegal Americans. He wanted to kick at something—anything—but he wasn't sure his sewed-up shoe would survive the impact.

"Hey, mister," a voice called to him from just past the park where the yacht *Granma* was on permanent display. It sat in a cage of glass panels, obscured and inaccessible.

Usnavy laid his eyes on a reedy boy with an original English-language Stephen King paperback in his hands and a worn green satchel at his side. The boy patted it lightly with his hands. "I got eggs," he said, "fresh country eggs." He quickly looked over his shoulder, making sure the sentries guarding the landlocked boat were far enough away so as not to hear him. Usnavy shook his head and the boy shrugged, indifferent or exhausted, and kept walking.

When Usnavy finally arrived at the bodega, the business day had started without him. They'd had an unscheduled delivery of masa carníca—a smelly, whitish meat paste the government was promoting for its nutritional value—and the lines curled around the block with people holding out their weathered ration books and used plastic bags. He saw his neighbor Rosita, surely there not for masa carníca but to get yet another blanket.

A couple of art students, with their long hair and haughty expressions (just like Reynaldo when he was a teenager), shared a book by Michel Foucalt in French while waiting, the pages torn and taped together. They went back and forth from Foucalt to a generic French-Spanish dictionary, equally beaten. A young boy in line with his mother played a handheld surely-imported-through-an-exiled-relative computerized war game.

In the meantime, the workers scooped and measured what little there was beyond the meat paste. More frequently they just shook their heads and lowered their eyes, like the guards at the museum/palace.

The scarcities were a daily shock that no one could get used to. The bodega had no eggs.

"Is everything okay?" asked Minerva, an elderly woman who'd been there with him every day since she'd started six years ago. They'd become friends instantly, bound by their devotion to the Revolution. She was one of the few good people left, Usnavy had remarked to Lidia not long ago. She understood her role, she understood her duty.

"Far more important than a good renumeration is the pride that comes from serving one's neighbors," she had said to him, quoting Che, when people began to scoff at them for their commitment, their adherence to the rules.

Now Minerva waited for him to answer but he was too distracted by recent events, by the turmoil in his belly and heart.

The truth was, Usnavy had never been late, had never been anything but early to any job, no matter how degrading or difficult. Even in Oriente, he'd always arrived long before the Americans showed up for their drinking and carousing, early enough to scout out his own position, to psych himself up.

Usnavy nodded at Minerva out of courtesy, even gave her a sallow little smile, but nothing was okay. He hadn't had his usual bite of bread, and not even that drop of coffee he'd needed so badly when he stormed out of his courtyard (now he figured the noise in his stomach would have to nourish him, his own saliva would have to satiate his thirst); he hadn't washed or shaved or brushed his teeth and he hadn't changed his underwear.

Most importantly, he hadn't talked to Lidia, hadn't patched things up with her from the night before, which made him vaguely nauseous. Because he'd left so quickly after getting up, he had no idea if she'd awakened with the intention of forgiving him, or at least pretending to have forgotten what had happened. Now he feared his silent departure would make her think it was he who was still angry. It would be more difficult now, he knew, to get over this unpleasant moment between them.

"How is Nena?" Minerva asked him.

"Nena?" Usnavy gasped. Did everyone already know?

Minerva nodded. "Yes, well, I was worried," she said a bit uneasily.

Usnavy retreated. His hands shook as he struggled to open a customer's plastic bag.

The rest of the day went by in a blur, until the line of customers became a sad trickle, the other workers went home for the afternoon break, and Usnavy was left by himself, sitting on a stool at the counter, his stomach tangled, staring at the foot traffic on the dusty street outside.

The world was sepia, warm but colorless.

Usnavy remembered when Jacinto first returned from Africa, how he was full of stories about wild animals and the flushed palette of the jungle. Then one night in a drunken stupor, when he was lamenting how his ex-wife had never understood him, Jacinto dropped a hand on Usnavy's knee and told him how, long ago in ancient times, Shaka, the Zulu king, encouraged his soldiers to have what they called *uku-hlobonga*—thigh sex—in order to keep them strong.

In Angola, Jacinto said, he had had extraordinary, energy-surging intercourse with a South African transvestite, only he didn't know at first she was a man.

"She wasn't like the locas here," Jacinto said. "She had lived like that all her life. Where she came from, in her tribe, if she acted like a woman, if she really believed she was a woman, well . . . she was . . . except for . . . you know . . ."

Thinking about young Reynaldo, who was always getting caught in women's dresses or in strange circumstances with older men, Usnavy had wanted to know more about how this could happen, how believing so much could transcend something so real, but Jacinto's fingers on his knee were beginning to travel and Usnavy had no interest at all in that. He took down the final swig of his own beer and, pretending he hadn't even noticed, stood up, causing Jacinto's hand to roll off.

"Aw, c'mon . . ." Jacinto whimpered.

It was 3 in the morning; Tejadillo echoed with a loneliness that Usnavy knew could be devastating. But there was nothing he could do to help his friend except give him a light punch on the shoulder and wish him easy dreams.

Now a drowsy Usnavy propped his head up with his hand, his elbow naked on the bodega's scratched and empty counter, stiff at the joint. Technically, the bodega was closed until 4 o'clock, but Usnavy was exhausted. He broke open *The Old Man and the Sea*. His hands hurt even as he turned the book's yellowed pages. His feet were burning and so he slipped off his shoes under the counter.

He knew that if he went home, he wouldn't have the strength to make his case to Lidia. His single consolation was knowing the broken lamp he'd found in the ruins—the Tiffany!—was safely hidden somewhere in the back of the bodega, stuffed in a cardboard box and wrapped in a blanket. He was certain no one at the bodega would ever grasp its worth.

Last night, standing over Nena and Lidia, he had finally and stubbornly checked the magnificent one for the signature—the T with the other letters hanging off it. He had climbed up on the bed and poked his head inside the lamp until it looked like he was wearing it for a hat.

Then he lowered the lamp, slowly, careful not to strain the chain or the electrical wires—though from the ceiling a fine grit rained on him and his family. When he concluded his search, he looked up and realized the hole from which the lamp dropped was bigger now, wider.

Yet he couldn't think about it right then, couldn't even consider the consequences because, once he'd had the magnificent one up close to him, he'd taken to it like an archaeologist might: with gentle care, with precision, but with a kind of focus that blackens away all else. He scoured every centimeter, with both his eyes and his hand—maybe, he considered, the initials were engraved but no longer visible. Perhaps they'd come up like Braille. But not even using a magnifying glass nor the bicarbonate of soda that Jacinto had once given him had helped Usnavy find what he was looking for. (All the while, he knew, Nena and Lidia were attempting sleep underneath him and the lamp, wordless and resentful.)

This was considerably more magnificent than any lamp he had ever seen—but, he admitted to himself with sadness, it was not a real Tiffany. Its creator, he figured, must have been a Cuban who didn't know what he was doing; another Juan Nobody who didn't understand that his talent was celestial but ultimately useless because it lacked a giant T to quantify and qualify it.

"Pssst . . . Usnavy . . ."

A sleepy Usnavy snapped to attention at the bodega counter.

"Usnavy, coño . . ."

It was Diosdado, standing in the middle of the street, his bifocals on the tip of his nose, motioning his friend over with a jerk of his head. He quickly looked over his shoulder.

"What . . . ?"

"C'mere," said Diosdado, his stubby legs planted stiffly, his impatient professorial air in full bloom.

Usnavy put down his Hemingway, ran his fingers through his white hair, and got up, sliding back into his shoes. His knees and elbows cracked, every juncture in his body yelled for grease.

"I'm getting old," he said to Diosdado as he walked around the counter to the middle of the street. The raw blister on his foot was rubbing against the leather, causing him to lean a little as he walked. If he had his bike, he thought to himself, he wouldn't feel this way. His limbs would be loose from exercise, his circulation would be flowing like the Nile. There would be no blister.

His friend ignored his complaint. "You drive, right?"

"Well, it's been a long time . . ." It had been years, decades even, since Usnavy had chauffeured Americans around Guantánamo, the only time he'd ever had behind the wheel of an automobile. It had been since before the Revolution, when he was just a boy.

"But it's just like riding a bike, right? You never forget?" insisted Diosdado.

"I . . . I don't know," Usnavy said.

"Look, Usnavy, I need your help." Diosdado didn't ask the way Obdulio had, impatient but as a friend. The manner in which Diosdado talked was almost a demand, defensive but proud. "It doesn't matter to me whether you approve or not, you can think whatever you want. I'm going to offer you money for something, okay? And you can accept it or not, think badly of it, whatever you want. But I'm going to do this—and believe me, if you don't help, I'll find somebody else who will. I'm coming to you first because of all the years we've known each other, and because—in spite of your stupid revolutionary purity—I know you need the money. For your information—okay?—I can hear your stomach grumbling during the domino games, and I'm sure Nena and Lidia's must be screaming too."

"What the hell are you talking about?" Usnavy demanded, hands on hips, indignant.

"I need a driver—you want to make some money? Real money? Dollars? I'll pay you to drive for me."

Usnavy shook his head in dismay and dropped his arms. "Diosdado, are you out of your mind or something?" he asked, now laughing sarcastically. "Did you lose your senses after that argument the other day, is that it? You think you're a foreigner or something? You don't have a car, my friend!"

Usnavy started to walk away but a determined Diosdado grabbed his arm and yanked him back.

"That's the car I need you to drive," Diosdado said, nodding in the direction of a white Daewoo parked a block away, near the Badagry woman's home. In that instant, Usnavy recalled *her* lamp—the one in the living room, the one her nephew had supposedly misplaced and Usnavy thought he'd seen over her shoulder—did it have a T anywhere on it?

"That's a rented car, Diosdado," Usnavy said, reluctantly setting thoughts of Tiffany aside.

"Yes, I need a driver for it. Will you do it?"

Usnavy squinted in the car's direction: It was certainly an expensive vehicle, he knew, with air-conditioning and tinted windows. He'd seen tourists pop open the back on cars like that and stuff in suitcase after suitcase. He always supposed they were en route to the airport, taking Cuba's trinkets and treasures with them.

"How'd you rent a car? What are you doing?" Usnavy asked. If it had been Frank, he'd have figured it was a scheme of some sort—he was always into money-making plots—but this was Diosdado, who acted responsibly nearly all of the time. Diosdado was insufferable, but of good morals.

"I didn't rent it. The person who rented it is a Canadian, a friend of my . . . of my . . ." Diosdado paused. His Adam's apple slung high and his dry lips seemed to open for an eternity, without sound, without breath.

Usnavy relaxed his own stance; it was a delicate moment and he didn't want Diosdado to pull away with one of his sudden outbursts. He raised his hand to his friend's shoulder and gave it a slight squeeze. "You okay?" he asked.

"Of course I'm okay!" Diosdado bellowed, offended, shaking Usnavy's hand off his shoulder. "Now are you in or what?"

The Daewoo was cramped. "If you can't drive, how'd you get it here?" he asked Diosdado as he struggled to fit into the driver's seat. He couldn't believe he'd agreed to drive a foreigner around—as if it were thirty-five years before, as if the Revolution had never taken place! What was happening to him? He'd closed the bodega down without even bothering to call someone to sub for him. *I'm just helping out a friend*, he told himself over and over, trying to be convincing.

"There's a little lever down there, under the seat, I think, which will move the seat," Diosdado said, leaning down from the passenger's side to the floor, tilting his head to better see through the lower half of his bifocals. He looked like a scientist, or an inspector.

"How'd you get it here?" Usnavy asked again, fingering the lever. He pulled on it and the seat suddenly plunged back, leaving his feet dangling off the pedals. Usnavy's stomach sloshed about. The sewed-up sole of his shoe snagged for an instant on the brake pedal edge but it didn't quite come loose.

"Ah, that's it . . . but you've got to bring it up a little." Diosdado ignored his friend's question yet again.

"Maybe if you get in the backseat and push me, I can get it to stay put a little closer to the pedals."

Diosdado popped his head up and glared at Usnavy. "Don't be such an underdeveloped moron, for god's sake," he said. "This is a First World vehicle. Do you really think someone has to climb in the back to push you in order to adjust the seat?"

"It's Korean or something," Usnavy snapped. "It's Third World, just like us."

"You know what I mean," Diosdado said. "Just pull the lever and bring yourself up. It can't be that hard!"

Usnavy tugged on the lever and scooted, letting the seat click into place. "Yes, I know exactly what you mean—which is that anything that's Cuban is difficult—anything that isn't Cuban is wonderful," he said, annoyed that Diosdado's instructions had worked.

"What are you talking about? Are you going to try and turn this into another Cuba-against-the-world argument—because I'm not ready for that, okay? Not now," Diosdado shot back, frustrated, as he quickly adjusted the passenger's seat. "Cubans don't make cars and have never made cars so there's not even a point of comparison, all right?"

"You know why we don't make cars?" Usnavy asked, his two feet desperately trying to remember how to handle the clutch and the accelerator and the brake all at once. If Lidia were here, he thought, she'd be giggling at his clumsiness. "Because we have allowed the world to think we can't make cars. I mean, why not? Why wouldn't we be able to make cars? Other small nations make cars—Japan, see, Korea and Italy, even the Yugoslavians. We could make cars if given the chance."

Diosdado rolled his eyes.

Usnavy turned the ignition only to have the engine grind so loud—it was like a drill, nails on a blackboard, and a squealing pig all rolled into one—that people on the street and nearby stoops shouted at him to stop. The Badagry woman and her two elderly widowed sisters peered out their barred window, a corona of light behind them. This would never have happened to Lidia.

"Oh my god! Oh my god!" screamed Diosdado, twisting in his seat as if he were having a seizure. "Do you have a clue what you're doing? Do you have a clue? Because if something happens to this car, Usnavy, I'm . . . I'm . . ."

"I told you it had been a long time, didn't I? Didn't I tell you that?"

Usnavy slammed his foot on the clutch and turned the key again. This time the engine purred and the neighbors smiled and clapped. But as soon as Usnavy tried to put the car in gear, it leapt ahead of him and died again. The neighbors chortled but for Jacinto, who walked by in such a hurry he didn't even notice it was Usnavy in the car. Diosdado groaned and slid down in the seat.

"Give me a minute, just give me a minute," Usnavy pleaded, turning the car on again. With his foot firmly on the clutch, he maneuvered the gear shaft through the diagram on the knob: up and down, then up to the right and down, then . . . His blistered foot slipped and the motor whined back to silence. Maybe, he thought, it was a good thing Lidia wasn't anywhere in sight, that way he wouldn't ever have to tell her about this. And certainly Nena could never know: What would she think of him?

"God help me," Diosdado said, his eyes teary behind his bifocals.

"Leave god out of this," Usnavy snarled, remembering the betrayal of light from the first three biblical days, turning the key and working his feet so that the Daewoo lunged forward, rabbit-like, hurling all his neighbors in Old Havana off the streets and stoops, but with the high-pitched sound of good-natured laughter trailing behind them.

Usnavy followed Diosdado's directions as best he could but Havana traffic was suddenly a horror to him. In Guantánamo a million years ago, there were only a few dozen vehicles and the population, he was certain, had respected stop signs and pedestrian crossings. Now, even in the very depths of the Special Period, Havana's streets—so pleasant and spacious on a bike—seemed a confused labyrinth. Everyone ignored even the simplest rules of the road. When Usnavy whirled the steering wheel at a curb to avoid hitting a handful of kids playing stickball in the street, Diosdado screamed.

"You're hysterical!" Usnavy yelled at him. "Control yourself—you'll only make things worse!"

Out of the corner of his eye he thought he saw the sparkly man from Lámparas Cubanas among the throngs leaping away from the Daewoo and was relieved to realize those had not been his chewed-up overalls floating off the Malecón. As the Daewoo careened down the block, the sparkly man, now holding his hip, turned and glowered in Usnavy's direction.

"Crazy old man!" someone yelled Usnavy's way. It was a man's voice he heard, but when he glanced in the rearview mirror there was only a statuesque mulatta, her figure shrinking in the distance, her wrists full of fantasy bracelets twinkling as she raised her fist to protest.

Finally on a straight-ahead course out of the city, Usnavy threw the car into fifth gear—he'd never, ever, driven a car with a fifth gear before—and settled back. Lidia would love this, he thought.

"You don't know how to drive," Diosdado said, curled into a fetal ball on the passenger's side.

"I'm driving, am I not?"

"You're like everybody else in this country, Usnavy, a braggart," Diosdado said.

"This is called driving, see?" Usnavy wiggled the wheel from side to side to show he'd gained command. The car zigzagged dangerously. "I may be a braggart but at least I'm not a coward like you. You're afraid of everything—you're afraid to imagine our greatness as Cubans because you can't imagine your own."

"Usnavy, what have we ever done that's great?"

"What . . . ?" Usnavy spun his head toward Diosdado—the car swerved—then back to the road. "Are you crazy? We have, first and foremost, set an example—"

"Oh no."

"Look, Diosdado, we have been robbed as a nation—everybody knows that! We have been robbed of opportunities, and we have been robbed of our real achievements."

"No, no, no!" Diosdado covered his ears; he'd heard it all before so many times.

"The Americans took away our war of independence from Spain," Usnavy said.

"Oh, please!"

"Alexander Graham Bell ripped off Meucci—"

"Who wasn't Cuban but Italian!" interrupted Diosdado.

"He lived here all his life, didn't he? Duchamp ripped off Picabia—" (This wasn't an argument either of them knew much about but they'd picked it up when Reynaldo had been a student at the Havana Art Institute and they'd since integrated it into their litany.)

"Who wasn't Cuban either but the son of some French diplomat stationed here."

"That's a lie!" screamed Usnavy.

"Picabia never even set foot in Cuba!"

"That's a lie! That's a lie! I suppose that next you're going to tell me Picasso didn't rip off Wifredo Lam?"

Diosdado sat up and turned to Usnavy. "I'll give you that one, okay? But what if Picasso hadn't ripped off Lam? What if Lam had been Picasso? Usnavy, look around . . . we're not big enough for a Picasso. What would we have done with that much greatness?"

When Diosdado and Usnavy arrived at their destination in Santa María del Mar, the beach was quiet and deserted. The water shone bright as a plate, flat and hard. As soon as the car came to a jerky stop off a park (as Diosdado indicated), a fresh-faced young foreigner looked up, delighted at the sight of them. He had been strewn on the grass, reading *Fodor's Cuba,* and rushed toward them like a gazelle.

Usnavy scrutinized the young man's well-toned body, fashionable haircut, and the multilevel sports shoes that gave his step such an unnatural spring. He was close to thirty, but his expression was as trusting and clean as a toddler's.

"This is Burt, a friend from Canada," Diosdado told Usnavy in Spanish. Then he said to the young foreigner: "*Uss-nah-veee.*"

Burt was wearing khaki shorts and a dark Polo shirt. Wrapped around his head were a pair of sunglasses that looked like diving goggles, they were so big and all-encompassing. Dangling from the tips around his ears was a neon-green string which dropped down around his neck. It was as thick as a shoelace.

Canadians, Americans: How could two peoples be so politically different and look so much alike? Usnavy figured, if American soldiers invaded Haiti they'd look as innocent and simple as Burt, who said something bright and fast in an incomprehensible English and stuck his hand out. Usnavy took it and felt the man's unexpectedly slippery grip.

"So what now?" Usnavy asked, uncertain, turning away from the American-looking Canadian to his friend.

"Okay, here's what now," said Diosdado, adjusting the bifocals on his nose and fingering his goatee like a wise old lecturer. "Our Canadian compañero first came to Cuba on a Jewish church mission."

"It can't be both Jewish and a church mission, Diosdado—you know better!" exclaimed Usnavy.

"You know what I mean," Diosdado said through clenched teeth.

"No, I don't."

"Yes, you do—he came with one of those groups that bring bread and medicine to the Jewish community."

"The Americans, yes."

"No, you idiot, the Canadians—the Canadians came first."

"Right, right," nodded Usnavy, glancing up at the strapping northerner, who smiled uneasily as the two old men argued.

"Now it seems he has fallen in love with a local girl," Diosdado explained. "She is an architectural guide, I believe. Her specialty is the Museum of the Revolution, before it was the Museum of the Revolution, back when it was the Presidential Palace. She talks to foreigners about the bullet holes from when they almost shot Batista, and the statues of Abraham Lincoln and the other heroes, and also about the chandeliers and cabinet work, all exclusively created by Tiffany & Company from New York."

Tiffany! Damn! The universe was just throwing Tiffany in his face.

Diosdado continued, oblivious: "He has visited her many times, on various trips, and now he would like to propose marriage—this, even though she is not Jewish."

Usnavy knew he was supposed to rejoice at the thought of love itself, and at the foreigner's appreciation of Cuban women, but he also knew romance had become a wicked thing in recent years: These days, love was more often just a strong desire to leave Cuba, a one-way ticket to anywhere but here. And as much as he tried to lift his lips in a smile, his eyes betrayed his sadness.

"Congratulate him, Usnavy, this is good news, remember?" Diosdado said, prodding his friend with a quick cuff to his empty belly.

Usnavy nodded in Burt's direction. "*Ber-ry gut,*" he said, ravages of his childhood efforts to learn that difficult and privileged tongue.

Burt's sunburnt face expanded into a wide grin and he went off on an unfathomable monologue about . . . *what?* The girl? Cuba? Marriage? Usnavy never heard the word love—he knew the word *love*—but English was something far away and long ago for him, and the Canadian talked so strangely anyway.

"Maybe he's a French-Canadian?" Usnavy asked.

"Of course not," said Diosdado. "Can't you tell the difference between French and English? We'd understand French, you cretin." Diosdado smiled deferentially at the Canadian as he insulted Usnavy yet again.

Usnavy cringed. Where was yesterday's defiance? Where was yesterday's resistance to foreign whim?

Then Usnavy recalled his own mother, back in Oriente, and how she'd gone from a headstrong, independent girl to a gracious and accommodating hostess in just a few years. He tightened his fists, just like Yoandry at Lámparas Cubanas, then remembered Lidia and Nena and forced himself to relax, to extend his fingers like spider legs, to stop thinking before he became completely immobilized.

When told about Burt's plan, it struck Usnavy as cowardly and unworthy of real love, but he knew there was no point in saying anything. For starters, he literally couldn't communicate with this gangly stranger. Moreover, what good would it do if he could? Would the Canadian listen to him? And what exactly would he say—that if he really loved her this was all a charade? That this kind of thing revealed more about him than anything they could possibly find out about her?

Usnavy had gone this far, all the way to Santa María del Mar, to earn a few dollars and see if, somehow—he realized this as he was driving, realized it only after he was already committed—he could buy a bike for his daughter (although he was also having second thoughts now, because he didn't want to inadvertently reward the awful incident at the hotel). He was too consumed with his own situation to worry much about some foreigner's intimate problems.

"Let me see if I understand," Usnavy said to Diosdado as they settled into the Daewoo again, the Canadian having folded his uncommonly large body onto the floor of the backseat. "We're going to drive by the girl's house to see if she's really home, like she told him she would be. That's all?"

"No, Usnavy, no," replied Diosdado, clearly irritated but trying to pretend he was calm for Burt's sake. "We're going to drive by so he can see her with his own eyes. She doesn't know he's here. We're going to drive by to make sure she's not going out with anybody else—that she's not out at parties or anything like that—so we need to do this very discretely. Get it?"

"If you don't understand English, then how do you know that's what he wants to do?" Usnavy asked Diosdado as he started the car. He felt the weight of the foreigner's bulk against the back of his seat. "I mean, this is pretty ridiculous."

"He's a friend of . . . he's a friend of Reynaldo's," said Diosdado. "My son explained it to me on the phone, before the Canadian got here. He has a whole plan. Now, c'mon, let's go." He pointed forward officiously, with an upturned palm, as if he were making an offering. He gazed out the window to the immense and placid blue of the ocean, then quickly at his shoes, with the most fleeting sideways glance at Usnavy before taking refuge back on the shore.

Okay, thought Usnavy, then Reynaldo's still Reynaldo—that's that. He'd have to tell Frank, even if there was no possibility of an apology, or of bringing Diosdado back to the domino game any time soon.

He slid the car into first, trying to calmly go through the other gears and not have the car vault down the street. But his first effort failed and the car died a terrible gnashing death, which caused the Canadian to pop his head up and say something no one understood.

Diosdado leaned back in his seat, gave a transparently fake smile to the foreigner, and, patting the air with his hand as if it were Burt's head, said, "*Soh-rrreee, soh-rrreee.*" Then he turned back and scowled at Usnavy.

Eventually, with Burt occasionally materializing to mime instructions for Usnavy (his wraparound glasses still on his head, neon-green shoelaces framing his face), the Daewoo began its afternoon of cruising. The girl, it seemed, was vacationing in Santa María del Mar and Burt was able to spy her instantly, sitting on the steps of a beach house not far off the road. The Canadian laughed nervously when he spotted her, rattling off what Usnavy and Diosdado presumed were pronouncements of love and admiration, then ducked down so she wouldn't see him.

But this time Usnavy picked up another word in the Canadian's verbiage, and it was as clear as the light from his magnificent lamp: Reina. He knew Diosdado heard it too, squirming there in the passenger's seat, his eyes shut so tight his lids trembled like the ocean before a storm.

The routine was simple enough: They drove by, confirmed it was still the same girl, and idled out of sight for a while. Then they cruised by again, pretending indifference. Sometimes, a middle-aged woman would stand at the door and talk with the girl; they figured she was her mother or an aunt. But mostly, the girl was alone or with a girlfriend, stretching, laughing, playing checkers, or gazing out at the world. This went on until dusk began to settle over the shore.

Usnavy couldn't tell much about the girl from behind the wheel. She was young, she had dark hair, like Nena. She had curvy hips and slightly bowed legs. Did she, like Nena, also need more than her parents could provide? Did she still know the words to "Tengo" or had she forgotten them by now?

Maybe she could tell him more about Mr. Tiffany, later, after this episode faded . . . Maybe, he thought, she would prefer to stay at the museum, with its hero's shirts and useless guns, rather than go north with the handsome foreigner. Perhaps the serenity of Canada could never mean as much to her as the din of Havana, with all its familiar anxieties.

"There's not that much traffic, you know," he said at one point. "Surely she's noticed us by now."

Diosdado shrugged. "Look, until he says to stop, we keep going."

Usnavy turned the car around again, barely paying attention anymore. They'd circled this finite piece of pavement so many times, there was no longer a thrill in shifting gears, the ride now as level and dull as the graying blue waters on the horizon.

In his boredom, Usnavy looked out for invading soldiers, spillovers from what he was convinced would be a massive assault on Haiti. If they came here, how many would be Cuban-born, or the children of exiles? Would Badagry's car-dealing grandson be among them, so long gone that he felt more at home on the other side than here, with them?

Or would he, upon landing on Cuban shores, see that those in the crosshairs were mirror images, brothers and sisters he'd recognize on sight and embrace? Would any of them, like the Canadian stowed away in the back, fall in love? That, he thought decisively, could happen too. And then what would they do?

Diosdado yawned. The sun was shivering in its descent, still robust enough to cause them to squint, but on its way down to a watery slumber.

Then it happened.

"Oh my fucking god!" Usnavy screamed as he slammed on the brakes, his eyes having drifted from the seascape to the abrupt sight of a young man standing smack in the middle of the road: The boy held his arms out as if he were Superman and could stop the Daewoo with his bare hands.

"What the . . . ?" Diosdado stuttered, his own arms up against the dashboard as Usnavy maneuvered and the Daewoo rocked in place, the Canadian rolling around in the back like a sack of grapefruits.

"Compañero!" shouted the young man. He was in his early twenties, cocky, muscular, wearing a tight-fitting green Polo shirt. He smoked a cigarette that he tossed to the ground as he swaggered from the front of the Daewoo to the driver's window.

Usnavy recognized him immediately. "Yoandry, what are you doing?" he asked. It was the clerk from Lámparas Cubanas. His greasy locks uncurled with the humidity, the acne on his face a rash of tiny scabs.

"You!" the clerk barked.

"You know each other?" Diosdado asked incredulously.

The Canadian poked his head from the back through the two front seats. "Hello," he said, slow and nasally enough that everyone understood. The neon-green strings coiled around his ears.

"What the fuck are you doing, old man?" Yoandry said, not paying attention to the Canadian and grabbing Usnavy by the shirt.

"Nothing," he responded, respectfully eyeing the hammy fist the boy had laid on him as well as the one that he was twirling in the air. Yoandry smelled so strongly of cigarettes that it overwhelmed the salt from the ocean.

"Just driving, like good citizens," a flustered Diosdado answered for them, smiling nervously, his voice cracking. "We're showing our friend here the beautiful beaches of our country." He pointed to Burt, who was now sitting up, but slanting forward in such a way as to hide behind the driver's seat and keep his girlfriend from seeing him.

Yoandry leaned in to look more closely at the foreigner and gasped. "Oh god," he said.

Burt grinned, embarrassed. "Sí, sí," he mumbled, managing to sound alien even in that simple syllable.

"You know him too?" a flabbergasted Diosdado asked.

"He's my sister's boyfriend," said Yoandry, disgusted. He let go of Usnavy but left his other meaty fist up on the windowsill for all to see. "What the hell is going on?"

"Ah, so you're her brother? How wonderful!" Diosdado chirped with another one of his patently false smiles, his voice unnaturally bright and cheery. "Burt here wanted to surprise your sister with his visit! Burt," he said, gesturing for the Canadian to straighten up, to get out of the car even. He signaled toward the girl. "It's her, yes, your love!"

Burt grinned like a fool, addressing Yoandry, who surprised Usnavy by responding in English—it was fractured, he could tell, it was all twisted metals, but it was English nonetheless and obviously functional.

"Okay," said Burt to whatever it was Yoandry had told him. "Okay," he said again, then yanked the door handle and, waving at his excited lover back at the beach house, struggled out of the car and dashed toward her. He had managed to produce a box of Belgian chocolates out of thin air that he now had tucked under his arm.

Diosdado leaned back in his seat, relieved. "Usnavy, let's park the car, let's stretch our legs, please."

Usnavy ignored him, turning to Yoandry instead, who was still standing in the middle of the otherwise deserted road: "Is your sister being true to him?"

"What?" The boy grabbed him again, this time practically pulling him out the car window.

"Usnavy! That's none of your goddamn business!" said a horrified Diosdado. Then, after a quick glance at Yoandry's fists: "Besides, of course—look at that girl! The picture of fidelity!"

But Usnavy was undaunted. He imagined them—him and the boy—as African warthogs, capable of killing even lions with their tusks, but convinced that in a fight among themselves there would only be shoving and snorting.

"Let go of me," he said, forcefully shaking the boy off and grabbing his wrist. "I asked for a reason, and it's not because I think your sister's a whore."

"You'd better let go—and you'd better talk fast, old man," Yoandry cautioned, pulling his arm back and aiming his fist even as Usnavy held on to the other.

"That foreigner, you know what he was paying us for? To watch your sister, that's what. So here's my advice: Whether he has a reason to worry is not my concern. But make sure that whatever is going on, he doesn't have a reason to think he should be concerned. Follow me?"

He wanted to add something about Yoandry's dishonesty at the lamp shop the other day, about the way he'd tried to trick him because of his ignorance, but instead, he let go of the boy's wrist. In this particular situation, he knew whose side he was on: Yoandry's sister, after all, was Cuban.

Diosdado held his breath.

Yoandry stared off at the foreigner, now on the steps of the beach house, making his case to his sister and offering her chocolate, piece by piece. He pondered for what seemed an eternity. "Okay," he finally said, lowering his fist. "I hear what you're saying, old man."

Then the boy pirouetted as if he were one of those herculean Russian ballet stars who no longer came to the island, and headed back to where the Canadian and the girl were hugging and kissing, celebrating their reunion.

Because Burt kept the Daewoo with him at the beach to drive his girl around, Usnavy and Diosdado were forced to walk back to Havana—a long, mostly silent march. The sky was a glorious red and purple behind them, the sea a bottomless blue that looked almost black, like the rich feline grays and purples on Usnavy's magnificent lamp at home. There was barely any traffic, and what few vehicles chugged by were jammed with other, earlier riders. Usnavy, his foot on fire, kicked at a small rock, which skipped ahead of him.

"Why'd you do that, huh?" Diosdado whispered, meaning not his friend's clumsy play but the way he had confronted Yoandry. Diosdado was tired, the skin on his face sagged, his goatee like a prickly cactus.

Usnavy shrugged. There was no way he could explain, not to Diosdado, not now.

"I don't know, I really don't know."

After the confrontation, a guileless Burt had paid them, Diosdado thirty dollars for coordinating the day, Usnavy twenty for driving. The single bill was folded in half in Usnavy's pants pocket. He had expected to feel excitement, a rush of hope—anything—if he ever made that much money, but instead he felt a strange, almost aching void in his chest.

"It just wasn't necessary," Diosdado said. He was practically gasping as they went up a hill.

Usnavy nodded and looked off toward the horizon, searching for paratroopers. There is not one other country in the world, he thought, that lives like we do: always looking over our shoulders, wondering if the black dot in the sky is an enemy plane or a bird. And the worst part was that if the invasion were here, on the northern shores of Cuba instead of in Haiti, he knew too well that there would be more than a few locals who would look over their shoulders as well, but mostly to see when they could feel free to cheer, when they could let loose with cries of hallelujah and hurrays.

"Do you ever think about Africa?" Usnavy asked suddenly.

"Africa?"

"Yeah, Africa."

Diosdado shook his head. "Can't say that I do."

"I do," confessed Usnavy, "all the time."

"You mean Angola?"

"No, no," said Usnavy, who had wanted to volunteer for that struggle but was kept from doing so because of his flat feet and back pain. "I mean, Africa—its vastness. Maybe it's because I'm part Jamaican, I don't know. I think about its destiny."

Diosdado said nothing.

"It's a curse, really," Usnavy continued. "Maybe the plagues, the famines—sometimes I wonder whether all that isn't the price of having once participated in selling its own sons and daughters."

Diosdado shook his head and kept walking.

After a while, they could see the outline of the city, a smoky crown on the water. Usnavy kicked at a small rock again, but this time his shoe caught on something and the sole flipped open, his toes caked, wiggling like greasy maggots. The dried blood from the blister was black.

Diosdado chuckled. His own shoes were a gift from his child, a pair of Reeboks that hugged his ankles and kept him steady. "My . . ." He glanced up at the city, with its huge swatches of absolute night from the government-imposed blackouts. "My son . . . you know, well, now . . . Reina . . . she—I'm still getting used to it—I'm not sure at all how I feel about any of this, you can't imagine, really . . . He's coming for a visit."

Usnavy swallowed hard. He knew better than to touch or even look at Diosdado now. He kept walking, putting one aching foot in front of the other, regardless of how unwieldy it was with the sole that now flip-flopped as he advanced.

"Well, that's good," he finally said.

"We'll see." Diosdado arched his eyebrows.

They were almost home.

"I really wish I had my bike," Usnavy lamented, sighing.

"Yes, yes," said Diosdado, putting his arm around his friend's shoulders.

IV.

The next morning, a depressed Usnavy tossed about on his crackling, leaf-thin mattress. Rather than lay in the dark, he'd turned on his lamp, its vivid colors spilling into the room, washing over him. Yet today there wasn't much comfort in the light: Instead of heat from the reds and imperial gold, he felt only the icy stare of the purples and whites. The feline eyes seemed to indict him in some way. Usnavy was strewn on his stomach, away from the lamp, resting his head in the folds of his arms. He hadn't shaved in two days and his face was stubbly, his armpits rancid.

Earlier, he'd heard the bustle of Nena readying for school, and Lidia carefully tiptoeing around him as she helped their daughter. But when he finally lifted his lids, thinking Nena would be gone and he and Lidia might finally talk, he discovered he was by himself in the darkness. Quickly, he turned on the magnificent lamp, as if hoping its beam would reveal Lidia's warm, doughy body hiding under a pillow or safely curled on the bed. But the light came cold this time, remote as a Saharan night.

When he looked up, he realized some of the lamp panels were dirty again and, grabbing his special silk cloth, rushed to polish them. On a few, a layer of moisture had turned the fresh dust from the hole in the ceiling into a sticky grime and Usnavy had to do some serious scrubbing.

When he and Lidia had first gotten together she told him he reminded her of Aladdin, rubbing on his lamp. But he couldn't see it at all—Aladdin's lamp had been an oil can, nothing more, and this was a piece of art, no matter its provenance.

Besides, it had never occurred to him in the past to wish for anything. As he buffed, being especially careful around the loose panels, he thought of everything that he had been wishing for lately—including his still fervent desire to accidentally bump up against Mr. Tiffany's signature somewhere on his lamp—and replaced it all with a yearning for reconciliation with Lidia, for peace with Nena, for Obdulio's safety so far away, for understanding between Diosdado and Reynaldo; as an aside, he wished for a box of Belgian chocolates. Then, as if unable to shake a newly acquired virus, he asked for a good pair of bikes to buy and, yes, for more dollars.

Usnavy stopped polishing.

His eyes stinging, he stepped from Nena and Lidia's bed to his own without letting his bare feet touch the floor (which looked wet anyway, although this could have been the screen of tears in his eyes) and lowered himself slowly to his ratty, newspaper-lined mattress. Then he cradled his head in his tired arms and sobbed.

Usnavy was lolling on the bed, his face streaked, when he heard a knock at the door.

If my anguish were weight, it would be heavier than the sand of all our beaches, he thought. *Where, now, is my strength? I have lost all my resourcefulness.*

The knocking continued.

"What?" he shouted, his voice hoarse. As if an echo, his stomach rumbled. He felt his guts twisting, pushing between the lining of his belly and the bed sheet.

"Usnavy?"

He flipped over. "Who is it?"

"It's Yoandry, and Burt—from yesterday."

What could they want? Usnavy asked himself, annoyed. He was thinking about not answering further, or telling them he was busy, when he suddenly realized they might be there to hire him as a driver again. Forgetting all his ambivalence, Usnavy leapt from the bed, his naked feet splashing into the cold puddle on the floor.

"Just a minute," he called out, cringing because of the water on his naked soles. He looked up for the leak but couldn't see anything through the light.

As he pulled on his crumpled and smelly clothes, he fingered the crisp twenty-dollar bill folded into his pocket. Looking around, he flipped the switch to turn off the lamp's bright beacon. In a flash, the tiny room went black, muted blues and pinks exploded in front of his eyes, and he leaned against the wall, famished, waiting a moment until the dizziness passed. Then he cracked open the door a tiny sliver, trying not to gaze directly into the brilliant blaze of day outside.

"I'm sorry," he said to the blank presence of the two men—Usnavy couldn't see them yet, his eyes still adjusting, "I was sleeping. What can I do for you?"

The two men looked like white globs, barely discernible from the sunlight. There was a movement among them, a slow-motion gesture of some sort, the sound coming from them like a dying tape recording.

"I told Burt about your broken lamp," said Yoandry. He was puffing on a hand-rolled cigarette that dribbled not just ashes but tobacco. As he spoke, he exhaled and used his fingers to extract bits of leaf from his tongue. "I think he might be willing to pay more than five dollars for it."

Usnavy said nothing. He was hiding behind the door, comparing the stink of his own body to the cloud of nicotine Yoandry always carried with him.

"You know, we could both make money off it . . . I'd get, you know, a commission," the boy said, but he was clearly anxious.

Just then a happy Burt said something and reached over to pat Usnavy's shoulder. The old man jerked involuntarily—just like Diosdado had done the day before—which startled the tall Canadian, causing him to back off and apologize. Usnavy understood *Soh-ree.*

"Hey, what's the matter with you?" Yoandry asked, showing his gritted teeth. He leaned in close to him, rolled up his fists automatically. His pimply face was a huge yellow moon. "Don't you realize this guy could mean a steady business for us?" But as soon as the boy got a whiff of Usnavy, he stepped back a bit and gasped for the less fetid air outside.

Usnavy shook his head, still trying to get his bearings.

"He's an antiques dealer—you understand? He runs a store with your friend's daughter's fiancé—talk about lucky breaks, huh? Don't ruin it for us, old man, this could be good for all of us. Now where's the lamp? He doesn't even care if it's broken."

"I don't want to give him a broken lamp!" protested Usnavy.

To everyone's astonishment, Yoandry aimed his shoulder at the door, but Usnavy was able to hold him back, pushing with his whole, tired body. Still, the boy managed a foot or two into Usnavy's room. "Holy shit—what's that?" he exclaimed, gazing upward. The magnificent lamp hung frozen and black above the bed.

"That's none of your business," said Usnavy, pushing the boy.

Yoandry turned and said something to the Canadian, who was all scared now. Usnavy could see him coming into view: Burt gaped dumbfounded at the magnificent lamp then made a nervous motion with his hand as if to say *Okay.*

"Listen, he doesn't care if the little lamp's broken," Yoandry insisted, turning to Usnavy. "And he'll buy that thing too," he added, pointing at the black dome behind Usnavy's shoulder. "Do you understand? He doesn't care. He'll pay us dollars, real dollars, enough for both of us—we'll split it evenly—for the little one, and god knows what for that atrocity."

Usnavy arched his eyebrows. "Your commission is the same as my fee? You're kidding me, right?"

The boy whirled his eyes, surveying the woeful tenement, then smugly aimed them back at Usnavy. "How else are you going to get any dollars at all, old man?"

Usnavy stiffened. "How else are you going to get anything that easy, huh?"

With that, he pushed the door even harder against Yoandry's shoulder, surprising himself by driving the muscle boy out of the room. As Yoandry pounded on the locked door and called his name, Usnavy felt around the darkness for his cot and threw himself on it. He thought his skull might explode from the pressure of so much hunger.

Usnavy's stomach was acting as if it were filled with snakes, all of them coiling, swallowing, strangling each other. The magnificent lamp was not for sale. The magnificent lamp was his own peculiar patrimony; it was all he'd ever had.

He reached over and pulled open the door of the small fridge, feeling its cool mist on his forearm and the gold of its tiny light. Maybe there was a bit of rice. He felt around without looking, then realized his fingers were knuckle deep in some kind of creamy liquid.

Usnavy sat up, his hand dripping on the floor and on his bed, and peered into the icebox. There, in plain sight, was a small blanket cut in pieces, marinating in a muddy sauce. It was the only thing in the entire fridge but for a domino-sized pat of margarine and two plastic bottles of soda, both filled with boiled water.

Disgusted and appalled, Usnavy slammed the door shut. The fridge rocked against the wall and let loose a blue spark. Had Lidia deliberately fed their daughter this . . . this *abomination*? Or had that cunning Rosita tricked her? Lidia, Usnavy knew, was a trusting soul. But still . . . Lidia had to know what was in her own refrigerator! She must have fallen under Rosita's spell, he determined, and imagined himself twisting Rosita's neck.

Usnavy wiped his hand on his dirty pants, then licked his fingers to get the last of it. It was good, he reluctantly admitted, his stomach looping. It was damn good . . . He sucked his hand clean and sat on the edge of the bed.

What to do?

He abruptly yanked open the door of the fridge and pulled out the pot with the blanket. He would not eat the blanket—he couldn't bring himself to do that. He would do this as cleanly, as stealthily, as a Maasai warrior sucking on a bull's jugular. He tipped the pot and sipped at its edge, drinking in the brown sauce. It had onions and tomatoes and maybe a bit of cumin. It was thick and tasty, with a hint of real beef. But then the blanket pushed up against his lips as he tilted the pot to get at the gravy and he grabbed it with his teeth, pulling and slurping to absorb as much of the nourishment as he could. He could feel the sauce messily trickling down his chin and neck; he was a hysterical hyena feasting.

After a frenzied moment, an agitated Usnavy regained his composure and shoved the pot into the fridge, the chewed end of a blanket remnant draped over its side. He was breathing heavily, as if he'd sprinted the length of the Malecón. He wiped his mouth with his forearm in one long, defeated gesture. He needed water; he needed a torrent to wash him away.

He turned on the light and went scavenging for clean clothes in his drawer. He had a couple of extra pairs of pants, and both were laundered and ironed along with a few T-shirts and regular shirts, all neatly folded next to his clean underwear in the drawer. Lidia, it seemed, must have forgiven him.

But to his dismay, the books piled next to the drawers under the bed were like sponges, watermarks crisscrossing their sides. After so many days of leaks and puddles, still no one had moved them. It was too late to save them now: Usnavy knew the covers would peel the minute he tried to separate them.

With the taste of the blanket lingering on his tongue, Usnavy grabbed what he needed, including his toothbrush, razor, and a plastic bottle filled with the last of the water from his barrel. He headed out across the courtyard to the communal shower, the twenty-dollar bill still hidden in his pocket. When he got there he found the drain stuffed up, and Chachi using bent metal hangers to pull out inky globs of sticky hair that looked like a mammoth black squid.

"This is gonna be awhile, compañero," Chachi said, barely glancing up at Usnavy. The frothy piles of hair sputtered on the floor next to him, rising and falling as if they were breathing on their own.

Usnavy's stomach turned ever so slowly. He looked over at the line of waiting people, everyone carrying their own modest toiletries and bottles or buckets of water. A couple of women worked at crossword puzzles in rolled-up magazines.

"The last one?" Usnavy called out. An elderly woman raised her hand and Usnavy nodded at her in acknowledgment. "I've got to lie down or I'll throw up," he admitted. "Is it okay with everybody if I go to my room and wait there?" The line muttered indifferently.

Usnavy trudged across the courtyard, the bottle sloshing the water around under his arm, his clothes draped over the other. He tried to imagine himself far away from Tejadillo, a fierce hunting dog among sleek Herero heroes relaxing in the hot springs between the mountains and Windhoek.

Usnavy had just reached his room when Jacinto came up behind him. "Usnavy, old man," he said, a little breathlessly, "can you help me?"

"What's the matter?"

"I need some food. For my mother. Anything."

As the grocer, Usnavy was used to people asking for food, for scraps, but Jacinto . . . never. Usnavy looked him over quickly, just enough to appreciate that all his usual swagger had dissipated. Before him was a once handsome russet-skinned man, his nappy hair like rotted cotton, his eyes wandering in an inner galaxy like satellites torn loose from their orbits.

"Are you okay?" Usnavy asked.

"My mother's gonna die, Usnavy," he said wearily. "I thought maybe . . . you might have something extra from the bodega, anything really. Whatever."

Usnavy hesitated. He had an awful, awful thought. "I . . . I have something . . . some meat, maybe," he finally said. "Just a minute."

He went inside and grabbed the pot from the fridge, covering it with his dirty shirt so nobody could see. They crossed the bustling tenement without a word, as people looked up from their card tournaments, board games, and other luckless entertainments, eyeing them suspiciously but not asking any questions.

Inside Jacinto's room, there was only a single, tiny bulb in a lamp covered by a silk shade with fringes. It shone white, like an oracle. The air in the room was pungent with the claustrophobic smell of disease. Jacinto had inexplicably put up wooden posts—like the kind crews contrived when buildings were unstable. Usnavy wanted to tell him this was a bit much on his part, that there were those invisible giants who held up the city, but just then he heard the even but fragile breathing of his friend's mother. Where was she?

A clothesline stretched across the room on which Jacinto had improvised something of a curtain with a frayed sheet. Behind it was a bed on which the old woman lay, still as soapstone. Usnavy felt sorry for her immediately: Shrunken, her bedclothes loose and damp about her, her dried up breasts testified to the many lives she'd nurtured.

Around her, the room was crowded with shelves full of religious icons, an altar holding dead flowers with papery petals, rotting bananas that leaked their puslike slime and harbored a haze of flies (why hadn't they eaten that fruit instead of letting it go to waste, marveled Usnavy, the gods would have surely understood!). Accompanying all that were a few photographs of once-upon-a-times: Jacinto's parents' wedding in elegant black-and-white, his mother a girlish bride; his father, a jazzman with a trumpet in his hand, hat rakishly tilted, the Eiffel Tower in the sepia background in the years when the Revolution was young and fresh and every Cuban was an ambassador; Jacinto himself, callow and fine, his bare and sculpted chest as much of a sight as the live lion he was crouching down to pat, somebody's domesticated but still dangerous pet out there in the jungle and war. In the picture, a massive AK-47 was strapped to Jacinto's back, its barrel aimed at the sky.

Usnavy knelt on the floor and, moving the shirt covering the pot into a bundle under it, put it down on a stunningly varnished mahogany coffee table. Jacinto winced and quickly slid a plastic cutting board under the shirt to protect the wood.

Usnavy couldn't believe what he was doing, couldn't believe he was suddenly no better than Rosita—in fact, maybe worse: She did it for money, he did it . . . for what? To seem generous? To seem good?

"Listen, Jacinto, this isn't really meat . . . it's . . . it's . . ." he began, but Jacinto surprised him.

"Soy, I know—don't worry," he said quickly, his eyes doing circles around the blanket in the pot as if to confirm that he understood that this was what they were talking about.

"No, no . . ." Usnavy tried to explain.

"Masa cárnica? No problem, my mother likes it fine," Jacinto said, his pupils now darting back and forth from Usnavy to the stirring on the bed.

"You know . . . ?" Usnavy asked, his voice trailing off before he could even finish his thoughts.

Jacinto reached into the pot and rolled a bit of the blanket in his fingers. Once he made a little ball of it, ripe and dripping, he placed it on his mother's mouth. Her tongue darted out and licked the juices.

Later that day, Usnavy found himself outside the giant colonial doors of the Fondo de Bienes Culturales in the Old Plaza, not far from the tenement. He cleared his throat and tried to figure out what he was going to say.

The plaza, which was all rounded cobblestones, was older than the cathedral, with a parking lot hidden beneath the neglected patch of pavement. Everything was made of stone, veined or stained with gray, all of it lost in the incandescence of the afternoon.

Usnavy had muttered to himself the whole way there about his stolen bike and eyed each one that pedaled by—Flying Pigeons and Roadsters and the occasional tourist-imported Trek—curious if the twenty-dollar bill now transferred to his clean pants pocket was enough to lure any of them from their sluggish, contented riders.

"I want my bike," he muttered. "I want my own damn bike."

Before walking over to the Old Plaza, Usnavy had washed up at Jacinto's, since he had a bathroom installed in his room. It boasted a portable shower with a small gas heater for his mother's comfort, and a flushing toilet and everything.

While he was washing, the twenty-dollar bill was concealed in the pocket of his dirty pants, which Usnavy kept in sight the whole time—a gesture that caused him some shame, because Jacinto had always been his friend and he hated that, all of a sudden, he had grown distrustful even of him.

As he bathed, feeling the warm water running down his body, his neighbor put his right shoe together again, this time using not just twine but some glue he'd gotten on the black market to fix his mother's furniture. It embarrassed Usnavy to only have one pair of shoes, but he knew his plight was not unique, just less common now, as the world turned upside down and the least likely people suddenly had Italian shoes for work and American loafers to hang around the house. (This was the case with Frank, who also had a pair of thick, flat German-brand sandals that molded to the very soles of his feet.)

"You can't nail into this wood," Jacinto said, done with the shoe and now patting his mother's battered bureau. It was a fine, dark caoba, burnished so that their faces appeared within its borders, like portraits drawn with gasoline. "It's hard as hell. I want to sell it to a foreigner. But I have to fix everything and polish it so it doesn't look like there was ever anything wrong with it. I ran out of the putty I had but I'll find some more, for sure."

Usnavy immediately made a mental note to bring Reynaldo—Reina?—whatever—and her/his fiancé to see Jacinto's things once they arrived in Havana. It was the least he could do. He would have considered bringing Burt—it's possible, if he was interested in lamps, he might be interested in furniture—but he wasn't sure he could get the Canadian away from Yoandry, who would surely try to usurp the deal.

The Fondo, which served as a kind of clearinghouse for craftspeople, was headquartered in a huge eighteenth-century mansion which once belonged to the Count of Mopox and Jaruco on the corner of Muralla and San Ignacio. At the beginning of the nineteenth century, the plaza had been an apex of culture: On the same block, the Havana Philharmonic had once made music, and not too far away the captain general's printing press had produced some early works. Now the plaza was windy and barren but for a few foreign tourists and a string of bare-chested kids who followed, brazenly begging for food or money.

Like the other manors on the plaza, the Fondo had great stone columns, with balconies amply described by Cirilo Villaverde in *Cecilia Valdés o la Loma del Angel*, the first real Cuban novel. The balconies—many crumbling and held up by wooden supports like the kind Jacinto imitated in his room—ran the length of four or five houses, the legacy of disappeared colonial millionaires. (Usnavy didn't argue about the need for these supports, but in his mind it was still the invisible giants leaning against the walls who ultimately made the difference.) These buildings had arched doorways with fan-shaped stained-glass portals above them. The glass in these was blue and white, remarkably insipid, maybe with a panel of burnt red here and there. Usnavy sniffed: The light that ran through them was merely tempered, never glorious.

During the years of the colony, the owners had lived upstairs in their dry serenity, sometimes with an occasional boarder or guest, but downstairs, in the shadowy and damp chambers, retail merchants—nearly all of them recent Spanish immigrants—would sell their cheap wares on portable tables, blankets, and display cases that could be pushed like carts. Standing there with the injured lamp in a brown paper bag in his hands, Usnavy felt a little like they might have, like somebody who had washed up on the shores.

"Excuse me," he said as he ventured toward a thin young man in a tie-dyed T-shirt and sporting a ponytail. The fellow was having a smoke and puttering outside the Fondo but exuded authority in a way that suggested he worked there. "I'm looking for someone . . . I don't know his name, he works on lamps."

"Lamps? Lots of guys work on lamps," the young man said with a lazy smile. "Do you know what kind of lamps?"

"Like this," Usnavy said, opening the mouth of the paper bag enough to let the injured lamp sparkle.

"Ahh . . ." the young man said, throwing his cigarette to the ground and grinding it out with his foot. Usnavy took note of his shoe: Its sole was multileveled, like Burt's. "This fellow always wears overalls? 'The reality of things is their light'—that guy?"

Usnavy had never heard the sparkly man say such a thing but it sounded right to him so he nodded.

"That's Virgilio," said the young man. "He's at his shop. Are you a private client?"

Usnavy hesitated. "I . . . I don't know, I just want to fix the lamp," he said.

The young man leaned over and peered into the bag again. "That could cost you. You just want light, right?"

Usnavy nodded again.

"Well, that's going to be expensive. If I were you, I'd get a new lamp, something practical, something more modern. That one's kind of ostentatious, don't you think?"

"You're probably right, yes," Usnavy said, trying to gauge his response. Was this guy trying to deceive him, like Yoandry that first day? "But I inherited this lamp from my mother, so it's got sentimental value," Usnavy lied, reducing his mother's gift to something so small, so unlikely. "You know how that is," he continued, his hand stroking the paper bag and clutching it tighter. "We become attached to things even if they're worthless."

The young man shrugged. He tilted his head and stared at his undoubtedly expensive American shoes. Usnavy could see him skipping across the sea in those things.

Virgilio—the sparkly man—lived a good way from the Fondo, up by the gleaming glass building that was the old American embassy, now officially called the U.S. Interests Section. It was one of the tallest, most modern buildings in the city. From the first haze of light in the skies each day, there was always a long, sullen line of visa petitioners stretching around it for blocks. The column was orderly and quiet but secreted an air of fatality as it inched forward. Even the small children hanging off their parents were unusually gloomy, everyone committed to giving up their memories of seashells and hurricanes and Revolution.

Usnavy walked gingerly on the shady side of the street across from them, prospective exiles who, at another time, would have been viewed as enemies or traitors. He couldn't begin to count how often he'd been called—and how often he'd responded—to repudiate and denounce a neighbor who'd decided to leave. At first, their flight was what he clearly perceived as betrayal, and his arm would be hearty and hurl eggs and tomatoes with the kind of fuel only rage can provide.

But later his body faltered, perhaps from old age, but more likely from the pain these constant losses caused him: Each time he pitched a rotting grapefruit or other piece of garbage at someone who had once been his friend—a boy he'd seen grow up in the tenement, a good boy, one of the sapos from the domino games; or a young woman who'd extended a kindness, perhaps with medicine for Nena, or a cold drink in her living room while he watched the Comandante on her TV; or someone who'd given Lidia a bit of oil or a candle—he felt weaker and weaker, until one day he went to one of those horrible encounters and could hardly move. As everyone around him yelled obscenities at the frightened elderly couple who'd scored visas to the U.S. (and whom Usnavy knew from the CDR itself, both former officers, competent and enthusiastic), he shuffled through the throngs, embraced them both wordlessly, and went home. After that, he never again allowed himself to be volunteered for that particular kind of activity.

Now, Usnavy saw Virgilio frown as he poked his head into the artisan's studio. Though the interaction at Lámparas Cubanas had been pleasant enough, it was clear that the more recent episode in which Usnavy had almost run him over in the Daewoo was still fresh on Virgilio's mind (tinted windows and all!).

"You nearly killed me," he said just as Usnavy tiptoed in. The door was held open by a block of blue glass that looked like a chunk of ice. Usnavy wanted to touch it but kept his hands on the paper bag with the injured lamp, gripping it a little tighter.

Virgilio's studio was an old stable turned into a garage in the back patio of a huge house that, like the tenement at Tejadillo, had been divided and subdivided until it was left with many single rooms. But to Usnavy's surprise, the only people he saw crossing the patio on his way to the back were old men and women, older than he in fact. A couple of the men wore yarmulkes, though they had no meaning for Usnavy. (The Jews he knew in Old Havana—usually called Turks and Poles by the Cubans—looked like everybody else.) There were no kids anywhere, not even around the domino game in the parlor that Usnavy stopped to watch for a moment before heading toward the rear. To his amazement, the elderly players maintained a complete and total silence; the only sound was the rattle of the dominos on the table, their little metal navels scratching its surface until it resembled nothing less than a tangle of wire and bars. In the meantime, a couple of cats looked on, snuggling together in the shade, bizarrely fat, oblivious to all dangers.

Facing Virgilio in the studio, Usnavy held the lamp like a baby. All around the artisan—again wearing his sparkly blue overalls—there were lamps, red and blue and orange panels, cooling on work frames, lamps drawn with flowers or trees, resting on shelves and in rows on the floor, lamps with seascapes and deep purples hanging by the dozen from the ceiling, though not one of them was turned on. Instead, just like at Lámparas Cubanas, they were bathed in the frosty filter of a long white fluorescent tube, plus whatever natural light leaked in through the windows. In the rear of the garage—in its day it would have housed about a dozen cars, one for nearly every apartment—there were piles of sand, metal benches, and a large contraption that looked like a cross between a furnace and a submarine.

Another old man puttered about, his face in the shadows. A younger man followed him. The two were stretching a large piece of something that resembled jelly, uncurling it from a folded position onto a large metal table. In the corner was what looked like a barrel with a smol-dering white fire. The two men did everything in silence, working like insects and balseros, but confident of their timing. Holding the piece with pincers, they carefully placed it in a giant metal box that looked like a refrigerator, then relaxed, slapping each other around in con-gratulation. The heat was unbearable but the two just wiped the sweat from their bodies with their bare hands, sputtering in the flames of the barrel.

"You were driving like a fool, like a maniac," said Virgilio, who was sitting at a table, pushing a piece of red glass under a stylus with a tiny diamond point and drawing a long, willowy flower into the surface. A thin hose attached to the stylus sprayed the point, the glass, and most of Virgilio's chest, which was protected by a black rubber apron. The wa-ter ran onto a pan and down to the floor, creating a giant black shadow on the cement; it was everywhere.

Virgilio's face was oval, a whirly knot on a tree trunk. His pupils were enlarged to macabre proportions by the glasses barely hanging on to the tip of his flat upside-down T-shaped nose. But he wasn't wearing anything other than his regular frames to protect his eyes. Even though he was annoyed and wet, his face and body continued to sparkle as if sprinkled with fairy dust.

Usnavy swallowed hard, hugging the injured lamp even closer to him. "I see you finally got your—what was it?—Armstrong 2401?" he said, nodding in the direction of the reddish glass. "American glass, right?"

Virgilio raised an eyebrow. "So you're a bad driver but a good lis-tener," the man replied, not even glancing up. "What can I do for you?" One of the domino-watching cats—the white one—came and pressed himself against Virgilio's leg, oblivious to the water, as if he didn't un-derstand his own species' natural aversion.

Usnavy couldn't help but look up and around. So many lamps! But not one of them was magnificent and so Usnavy had secondary, conflicting emotions: On the one hand, that they hung there in varying states of completion meant that orders kept coming in before Virgilio could finish with one or another; but, on the other, if there were so many already available, the wounded one he was nursing wasn't that special after all.

"It must be peculiar to live so close, huh?" he said, pointing with his shoulder in the direction of the American quasi-embassy. His face was also wet now from the heat, slippery.

Virgilio shrugged. The other cat, a mustard-colored brute that looked like a lioness, trailed in, sniffed at Usnavy, and turned away unimpressed.

"I mean, I don't know . . . all that sadness," Usnavy said. His shirt sucked onto his back, soaked.

Virgilio frowned again. "It's always been like that," he said. "Always."

"Yeah?" Usnavy felt perspiration collecting in his solar plexus, a river down to his waist, tickling his navel. Cubans had always wanted to leave? *Always?* That couldn't be true.

"Sometimes longer, sometimes shorter, but there hasn't been a day since 1951—that's when I first moved here—without a line out there," Virgilio said. "The rest is lies, politics, and fable."

Usnavy nodded out of courtesy. "'The reality of things is their light,'" he said sheepishly while wiping his face with his hand, which dripped as it crossed his line of vision.

Virgilio finally looked up. He squinted at Usnavy, as if whatever he was giving off was too blinding to face straight ahead. "You don't read Thomas Aquinas," he said, not a question or accusation, but a simple statement of fact. His two assistants were now poking the barrel with a long metal pipe, the young man watching as the older one twirled the pipe between expert fingers.

"I read Fanon, I read Soyinka," Usnavy responded, flustered. His buttocks were drenched, his underwear clinging to him like a second skin. "And Hemingway, of course."

"But not Guillén and Langston Hughes?" Virgilio finished his engraving and lifted his foot from a pedal Usnavy hadn't noticed before. The diamond tip went limp, the water a trickle.

Usnavy sighed. "Of course Guillén and Langston Hughes. I meant beyond that."

"But you're not interested in light, not really," said Virgilio. "You're interested in glass." Then, without hesitating: "Is that the same lamp I saw the other day?" The snow-colored cat curled into a ball, its whiteness challenging the block of blue at the door.

Usnavy nodded as he handed Virgilio the bag. "Is that really true," he asked as the artisan pulled the injured lamp out to the light, "that there's been a line out there since 1951?" He gazed meaningfully in the direction of the Americans.

"Uh huh," Virgilio answered while examining Usnavy's lamp again. "Maybe even before that. But certainly longer than 1959. Now, tell me something."

"Yes." The heat was making him dizzy, the tracers orange and pink.

"Since I already saw this lamp and gave you a recommendation—a recommendation you can't afford—why would you bring it back?"

"I felt," said Usnavy as he took a long and labored breath, watching while the old man in the back blew into one end of the pipe and the other end grew into the color and size of an avocado, "that there was something you weren't telling me, that maybe you couldn't tell me . . . there."

Virgilio leaned back and arched his eyebrows. He scratched the mustard-colored cat's neck, leading him to purr so loudly Usnavy was initially startled. But after a pause, Virgilio vigorously shook his head, causing a light shower of sweat that the cat, inexplicably, didn't seem to mind.

"No," he finally responded. "I said all I had to say then. Maybe it's you who has something to tell me."

After his unproductive visit to Virgilio's infernal studio—the man wouldn't fix the lamp without payment of at least the twenty-dollar bill in Usnavy's pocket, nor would he consider buying the lamp—Usnavy walked over to the hospital to see about the number on Nena's birth certificate. Earlier, while washing and dressing, he had confided to Jacinto what had happened at the Habana Libre and he was surprised by his friend's rather mild and sensible response.

"She's a kid, Usnavy," he'd said while fixing Usnavy's shoe again. Jacinto's mother lay quietly in her bed, flushed and satisfied. "You're lucky that's all that happened. Thank the saints, my friend—she's not pregnant, she didn't get caught stealing or leaving the country. All kids rebel, that's what they do, old man. C'mon, how long has it been since you were a little wild? All kids are a little wild."

Usnavy struggled to remember when he'd been a little wild . . . maybe back when, as a boy, he'd steal picture books and comics from the foreign men who came to sit in his mother's parlor and then, after he'd finished looking at them—he really couldn't read them, they were in English anyway—he'd return them, sometimes a little worn, sometimes a little smudged, but always whole.

Usnavy was crossing the street to the hospital, barely looking at traffic as he tussled with his memory, when he almost ran into the boy from the previous morning, the one who'd explained to him about Ja-cinto's ex-wife and the brujería.

"Hey—*hey*—watch it, old man," the kid said. He was wearing what looked like a dozen black hula-hoops around his neck.

"Sorry," Usnavy answered, scarcely looking up, until he realized what it was the boy was carrying. "Eh . . . whoa, wait a minute." Usnavy ran across the street after him, his knees popping and cracking with each step. The blister on his foot had swollen and broken open again from so much walking. He limped and cringed and cursed under his breath. The broken lamp, still in the sack, rattled a little. "Those are bike tires?"

The kid kept walking, eyeing the jingling bag and the old man sus-piciously and nodding with disdain. "Yeah. So?"

"So I need a bike," Usnavy said.

"So?" the boy retorted even more insolently.

"So you've got bike tires, I need a bike . . . What I'm asking isn't so difficult to decipher," Usnavy shot back, impatient now.

"Aw, you're too late. I sold mine already. So you see, I can't help you, old man, I'm out of here."

Usnavy was panting as he tried to keep up with him. "What do you mean you're out of here?"

"I mean, I'm gone, old man, gone!" he said with a grin that filled up his whole face. "I'm on my way to La Yuma!"

"Wait a minute—wait a minute!" Usnavy snapped, grabbing his arm. The bike tires tumbled from the kid's skinny frame, trapping him at an angle, encircling him mid-torso but for Usnavy's strong fingers. "What the hell do you mean?"

"C'mon, old man, you know what I'm talking about—everybody knows you helped your friend Obdulio," the boy said, shaking him off and grabbing the tires like the hem of a colonial-era skirt. "Listen, the coasts are wide open, they're letting everybody go . . . People are even leaving right from the Malecón. How long can that last, huh? I've got to take my opportunity."

Usnavy was stupefied. "Everybody knows . . . ? They're leaving from the Malecón . . . Wait—what about your parents? Your family? You're just a boy!"

He was even younger than Nena! What was going on?

The kid shrugged and laughed and ran along. "I'm going with Chachi and Yamilet—I'll send you a postcard, old man!" he yelled over his shoulder as the bike tires danced about him.

At the hospital Usnavy could barely concentrate. He was told to go upstairs to the records office but he kept wandering into lightless rooms where long lines of patients waited with wide-eyed, resigned faces. They didn't look much different than those curling around the U.S. Special Interests Section, their lives in the balance.

There was a handwritten sign on the elevators: *Reserved for Patients Only.* Usnavy counted steps as he went up in order to keep himself focused. *One, two, three, four.* He'd heard that this was a good way to concentrate; you could see a lot of seniors in Havana now, veterans of those early-morning open-air Tai Chi classes, going about their days counting everything from the cracks in the sidewalks to the liver spots on their hands. Usnavy held the injured lamp under his arm and strained as he took the steps—*fifteen, sixteen, seventeen*—imagining himself at the local park, doing stretching exercises with widows and lost men.

On the second floor, he found himself in a shadowy hallway turned into some sort of office where a few solemn-faced nurses scribbled by hand. Their work was tucked into file folders piled high on a table. One of the nurses appeared to be on break, smoking, with a severe look

ACHY OBEJAS ❧ 149

on her face as she played solitaire. Another nurse was talking on the phone, giggling and gossiping.

After inquiring about hospital records and waiting for what seemed an infinity, yet another nurse—she barely looked at him—led Usnavy down an even blurrier hall to a room full of books with yellowed pages. She deposited him there, turned, and closed the door behind her, leaving Usnavy and his broken lamp all alone. Here, even the floor had stacks of dusty books everywhere, the result of prior visitors too lazy or in too much of a hurry to put them back in any kind of order. It occurred to Usnavy that, alone, he could embed secret messages in them, tear the books to pieces, pee on their pages, or set the room on fire. If only he were capable of any of it, he thought, if only . . .

He sat down at the only table under the nervous flickering of yet another long fluorescent tube. He placed the broken lamp carefully on the floor beside him, then ran his hand through his hair and sighed.

"Okay," he said aloud, "okay."

Then he pulled the first heavy tome toward him and began to strip the flimsy pages one from the other, searching for names corresponding to 1980, Nena's birth year and the last time Cuba had experienced a mass exodus. He remembered thinking at the time that it would never happen again, that this tide of people leaving couldn't be more than this one explosion, and that Nena's arrival was not just replenishment but also a rebirth, a new dawn, with its subtle rainbows, its dignity and glory. He wanted to return to Cojímar, to call everyone back from the lure of the lights on the other side.

Our fate, he thought as he turned the pages, *can't be to suffer these constant losses.*

Usnavy stared at the scores and scores of names, at the hundreds of Cuban births on the page in front of him. And in a second, he saw them all: Cubans on the bounding sea, Cubans at sunrise and dusk; multitudes of Cubans before Che's visage, wandering Fifth Avenue or the Thames, the shores of the Bosphorous or the sands outside the pyramids; mirrors and mirrors, mercury and water; a family portrait in Hialeah that he recognized from years before in Caimanera; the thick green leaves of tobacco and forgotten stalks of cane flowering in the fields; his mother with her tangled hair, his father tilting his hat like Jacinto's father but in New Orleans or Galveston; the shadows of birds of paradise against a stucco wall; ivory dominos; a shallow and watery grave, then another longer passage, a trail of bones back to Badagry; bison and cheetahs.

As he went from page to page, Usnavy fingered the lamp in the bag and realized Virgilio was right: He was engaged not by the reality of light, by its brilliance or heat, but by the universe of colors in his magnificent lamp—the one in his room, the spectacular one with no signature—by the bubbles and ripples that marred certain panels but which he had grown to think of as particularities, not imperfections; all parts of the greater and more beautiful whole.

He knew his great lamp by heart: the panel with a wave, the one with effervescence; one for sure had a hairline—or a hair itself, perhaps. Some were thicker, bolder than all the others. He knew each curve and slope, each flat surface, each sharp grain. They were flawed but steady, genuine, *his*.

The reality of light for him was precisely this: The surfaces on which it glittered, the scenes it illuminated. Light alone was air, nothingness.

And glass, he knew, was not what it seemed. It was solid to the unknowing eye, but Usnavy understood the atomic structure belied its true identity, indeed, its DNA. Glass was liquid, just like rain, like the ocean, like the water embracing his beloved island.

* * *

For hours, Usnavy searched through tome after tome for Nena's number. In all of that time, no one came looking for him; no one even peeked inside the room. It was all silence and stillness, a place without time or day of the week, a room as empty or full as he wanted it to be: the hull of a ship, the cabin on a space rocket, a womb. What could the Leakeys find here?

There are no wild animals in Cuba, Usnavy thought as he hunted, none. "No wild animals here," he muttered to himself, "only anteaters, transparent frogs, and tiny, tiny birds. No bears, no lions, no tigers, not even a sighting, a description of one."

Horses came with the conquerors, cats with the slaves, and the Taínos and Siboneys, he continued to himself, died from too much smoke. The Jews came to Cuba in disguise looking for salvation, the Chinese for gold mountains and silver fish, and the Africans—dragged here against their will—prayed that the island was at least less savage than those beasts that pretended to own them.

Usnavy couldn't believe it. He'd found the right book, found the right page, except Nena's number wasn't there. The page followed its sick linear logic, one little numeral after another, but there, where Nena's number should have been, next to her name, next to his and Lidia's, was instead a gap, a tear, a hole in the page, as round as a pen, as charred at the edges as a bullet wound.

Usnavy grabbed his lamp from the floor littered with dusty books and explained this all to the nurse who'd just reappeared. She sighed as if she'd accompanied her widowed mother to those Tai Chi exercises and had learned to hold all the air of the world in her lungs and to let it out so slowly that hours would pass and she'd still be standing there, in the perfectly tranquil garden of her mind, her lips slightly puckered, the air hissing its last.

"No lions," Usnavy grumbled as he waited for her to take it all in and decide what, if anything, to do next. He wanted the invisible giants to take him away to a cozy and quiet place where he could go to sleep, a deep, deep sleep.

The nurse gave him a quick glance, as if she wasn't sure what she'd heard—*lions?*—then led him down another infinite abyss of a hallway to yet another room, a vault full of mildew and silence. Usnavy shivered. She didn't turn on the light but sauntered to the center, as if it was a temple and this was the bima or sacrificial rock. After a flick of her wrist Usnavy saw a tiny point of light explode in the middle of the blackness: a star burst, an official form—another form!—taking shape on the blue screen.

"Her name?" the nurse said.

He gave her the information all over again, this time noticing that, as he waited, his feet made a squishy sound, a wet smacking sound like kisses. He looked down at the impossible blackness around his shoes, then up at the nurse, who was nothing more than a perfect silhouette bent over the computer keyboard.

"The floor's wet," he said.

She nodded, maybe—he couldn't really tell—and kept typing.

"With the computer . . . I mean, you could get electrocuted," he went on. He had the injured lamp in the dry paper bag under his arm.

"There's a leak," she said, ignoring him.

A leak? There was water everywhere. Usnavy felt his heart split open like a fleshy green coconut.

By the time he got to Tejadillo, Usnavy had not only skipped the morning shift at the bodega but was on his way to blowing off the afternoon too. He knew this would be the second time in so many days that he'd missed work and, undoubtedly, there would be worry enough to send someone to his house to see what was wrong. But for the first time in his life, he didn't care. What could they say to him? That he was like everyone else? What could they do?

Usnavy pushed his way through the courtyard where his neighbors were brazenly preparing to flee the country, their ropes, plastic jugs, and junk collecting in the middle like the stuff for a bonfire. Instead of the clanging cymbals and braying trumpets of timba, now the courtyard echoed with the wail of recorded electric guitars and their promises.

Usnavy elbowed past the kids who ran around handing the adults bags and knapsacks and pieces of wood, metal hangers like the one Chachi had used to unstuff the drain, and belts and ropes to hold things together. (Instinctively, he looked around for Nena, relieved to not find her among those preparing to leave.) The mood was festive, like a balloon, and as fragile: This could turn into shreds of meaningless rubber, into nothing, if anybody took it that wee bit too far. No one was playing dominos or marbles or Parcheesi now. A frayed poster from a previous holiday march flapped from a balcony above, its red letters quoting Che: *We cannot be sure of having something to live for unless we're willing to die for it.*

Usnavy threw open the door to his family's room in time to catch a startled Lidia and Rosita in the very throes of their own crime: The aroma of tender meat filled the room. Usnavy gasped. Sitting on the floor, the women were holding above an iron pot various blankets, all brown with spices, cutting them into strips that resembled beef. High above them the magnificent lamp shone like the arrival of fair-haired Columbus before the island's natives: effulgent, imperial.

"Where have you been?" Lidia demanded, leaping from the floor but not even pretending to cover up her activities.

"Where have I . . . ? What are you doing?" he cried.

Lidia stiffened. "We're earning some dollars," she said defiantly. From the floor, Rosita smirked, her hands stained gold from their labor.

"You fed this to our daughter!" he exclaimed, his teeth clenched, pointing with his nose like a hunting dog at the strips coiling in the cauldron. They swarmed around like intestines, like worms.

"No, no, no, Usnavy, it's not what you think," Rosita rose to his wife's defense, all the while wiping her hands on a rag.

"Stay out of it!" he screamed.

"Stay out of it? Thanks to her our daughter has vitamins, Usnavy!" Lidia hissed. She grabbed a white medicinal bottle from on top of the fridge and shook it in his face, its pills like seeds in a maraca or chekeré.

"You fed our daughter a blanket, Lidia, how can you even talk about vitamins?"

As he fretted, Rosita maneuvered behind him and closed the door, where a few of the courtyard kids had begun to peer in, drawn by the spectacle of an argument between a couple that wasn't known to fight. The neighbors' eyes were larger, more intense, and precarious than the cats' above.

"What about that, huh?" Usnavy ranted.

"I tell you, she didn't know!" Rosita hissed. "I sold her the damn sandwich without her knowing what it was."

"But when I found out, I asked in," Lidia continued, without apology. "I mean, somebody here has to earn some dollars, Usnavy, and it wasn't going to be you!"

"Oh yeah? Oh yeah?" Usnavy tossed the injured lamp down on the bed, its brittle pieces rattling and clanging in protest, and pushed his fists into his pants pocket. "You'll see, you'll see!" he railed, pulling both his pocket linings into the light, fuzzy sock puppets that dangled from his waist, flaccid and empty. "What . . . ?"

He thrust his palms into his back pockets, pulling those free as well, the twenty-dollar bill nowhere to be found, while Rosita and Lidia gave each other worried looks. "It's here, hold on—I had a twenty-dollar bill—dollars—I had them just two minutes ago," he protested as he frantically patted himself on his chest and thighs. "Maybe that nurse . . . that fucking nurse . . ."

The scrap of paper on which Nena's temporary birth certificate number was written rolled from a fold in one of his back pockets and he scrambled to the floor eagerly, then, realizing what it was, tossed it on the bed. "Your daughter's birth certificate number . . . well, this one's just until they find the real one . . . see? It's here, I'm placing it right here," he said deliberately, theatrically, his hair tossed all about, as he tore at Nena's Michael Jackson poster—Lidia and Rosita cringed at the sound—leaving one gigantic jagged scar of white across it. He fumbled with the piece of tape on the poster's back, then pulled it from the paper. The gumminess glued his fingers together unexpectedly and he jerked his hand for an instant, sticking the tape on the wall, the birth certificate number clinging to it.

Usnavy was panting. Perspiration trickled down his face, cold and clear. "Somebody stole my money," he said, thoroughly defeated. "I had twenty dollars—I drove a Canadian around and made twenty dollars—"

"You drove . . . ?" Lidia said, amazed. "A foreigner . . . ?"

"You can ask Diosdado—you can ask Jacinto, he saw my money—goddamn it, goddamn it, goddamn it!" He was pulling his hair.

Rosita shook her head. "Salao," she whispered, grabbing her pot of fake meat and trying to slip out the door. "I've got to run," she said to Lidia, "before no one can get out."

"Salao, huh?" screamed Usnavy. But his voice squeaked and cracked—in the chaos, he remembered a verse from the Book of Amos: *Does a lion roar in the forest when he has no prey?* "I'm so goddamn sick of being salao!" he yelped.

And with that he shoved Lidia against the door, making it impossible for Rosita to escape. He leapt on the bed, taking hold of his magnificent lamp with his two flinty hands. The lamp groaned and dropped another inch from the ceiling, raining down its wheezy white meal on Usnavy, who seemed not to notice that his prize now hung by the miracle of a thin knot of red and blue wires intertwined like cardiac arteries. As the two women watched dumbfounded, Usnavy snapped a red glass panel out of the lamp, then another.

"See these? See these?" he shouted at them, one panel like a fiery flame in each fist. "I'll show you who will bring the dollars to this house! I'll show you who's salao!"

Then he hopped from the bed, his right shoe inexplicably flipping open, and ran out of the room, out to the courtyard where Chachi and Yamilet and the boy with the bike tires were tying together the handles of bulging plastic bags to take on their journey. Usnavy rushed past the swarming flies by the deserted bathroom, past Jacinto's clean and varnished door and the noise of radio and TV broadcasts in a babel of languages he couldn't understand, out to Tejadillo, now as rude and jammed as if it were market day in Dakar or Lagos.

V.

In the north of Africa—in Egypt—a sculptured tomb found in Memphis features carved yellow-brown human figures blowing glass, the crystalline globes at the end of their long pipes dangling delicately in the air. Scattered about are 4,000-year-old glass beads, glass scarabs, glass amulets, glass pieces for games no one's been able to decipher and play.

In Sidar, the capital of Phoenicia, the rulers had special sand brought in from Mount Carmel just for glassmaking. But the first manufacture ever of colored glass—the kind that would lead to Usnavy's magnificent lamp nearly a millennium and a half later—occurred in China, the birthplace of dominos, when the Emperor Ou-Ti established a factory to make rods of tinted beads and other glassware.

That's all gone now, their existence as things of beauty in ruins, alive only in the collective imagination, in the same way that fossilized teeth from Aramis and Kanapoi evoke primitive man/monkeys with their sloping foreheads, inculpable and extraordinary, the unlikely progenitors of Mandela and Madame Curie, Lenin and Lennon, José Martí and Celia Cruz.

But when Usnavy burst through the door at Virgilio's, he wasn't thinking about any of this. He had run—sprinted, each leg bending and stretching, sinews expanding and contracting—through the streets of Havana with his two red panels like lumps of burning coal fused into the very fiber of his fingers.

"What the . . . ?" Virgilio leapt from his work bench, surprised and frightened, his eyeglasses slipping from his flat upside-down T-shaped nose, not shattering on impact with the concrete floor only because of the many layers of newspapers and cardboard that cushioned the dozens of lamps all around him, each one staring unabashedly at Usnavy.

"Armstrong? Are these Armstrong? Are these American glass?" a winded, spent Usnavy asked, his arms outstretched and shaking.

A concerned Virgilio pried the panels from Usnavy's hands— searing red, they looked like bloody blades, like something criminal. The minute his fingers were loose, a sweaty, dizzy Usnavy spasmed.

"Let me see," Virgilio said, turning away in a slow, deliberate manner, making sure there were no sudden moves, no causes for alarm. But Usnavy followed him up close anyway, placing his damp, anxious face above Virgilio's shoulder as soon as the artisan sat back down. "Give me some room." Virgilio gently pushed Usnavy away. "You can watch from there but I need to see these in the light." There was no one in the studio but them, the barrel of fire in the back just a can of embers now, the heat simmering, tolerable.

Usnavy moved a bit, rattling a lamp on the floor next to him, startling the snow-white cat, which disappeared like a jolt of light, like the tracers Usnavy saw when he was overwhelmed by hunger.

"I appreciate you bringing these to me," Virgilio said as he picked up his glasses from the floor and fumbled to put them on his flat, whirly-knot face. "But I don't want you to get too excited. Armstrong is hard to find in Cuba. And in the end, you know, I can work with anything— stained glass is just regular glass colored with oxides and chlorides, then ground up with the right fluxes and fused into the surface. We blow a lot of glass ourselves right here, we recycle a lot—Armstrong would be nice but we don't really need it, you know what I mean?" He adjusted his glasses, settling in to examine Usnavy's treasures. Virgilio was, as always, sparkling, twinkling all over, like a comet or a falling star. "It's the design, the artistry, which makes a difference. Sometimes when we're lacking in imagination we blame the materials—our egos are too big, I think—but a true artist works with anything." He coughed, looked around as if searching for the gaffers, anyone. "And anyway, let's be realistic: This isn't really art, this is more like an auto shop. I fix these things the same way some other guy fixes a DeSoto or a Ford. Except that he's doing something for his compatriot, and me, I'm mostly working for the English, you know what I mean?"

Usnavy leaned against the door, his leg trembling like Yoandry's that day at Lámparas Cubanas. He hated that expression—*working for the English, working for the Man*—the English had been in Cuba for only a blink of time and, in his mind, they'd done more good than bad. Who else could they say that about? The Spanish? The Soviets? The Americans who were everywhere but pretended to be nowhere, always igniting fires they then came rushing to put out, demanding payment for service or, worse, hero's medals?

At his worktable, Virgilio examined the red panels with care, touching, staring, putting them under a magnifying lens. At one point, he put each in his sparkly palm, feeling its weight, then limped out to the patio—Usnavy at his heels, limping too from his blister—and looked at them in natural light. He stepped aside and probed the way light itself performed as it filtered through them. Red danced on the broken tiles, made the mustard-colored cat glance up from his regal nap and sniff the air.

"Where did you get these?" Virgilio asked, clearly astounded.

Usnavy shrugged. "Your cat," he said, avoiding the question, "it looks like a lion."

Virgilio ignored him, lost in the texture and power of the two red panels. "These are . . . well, *interesting*," he said.

"Can you . . . can you tell where they come from?"

"Where they come from? What do you mean, where they come from?"

"I mean, you know, who made them, how old they are, that kind of thing," Usnavy said, a bit flustered.

Virgilio shook his head. "You can't really date glass, it's got no carbon in it. Sometimes you can tell something by the color—you know, certain colors didn't exist before certain periods of times. We know that gaffers didn't invent certain formulas until later. Other than that, well, unless you know the chemical formula you're looking for, and unless you take a little piece of the glass you're trying to date and grind it down so you can get somebody to do a chemical analysis, well, my friend, it's pretty much impossible."

Usnavy pondered. "You have to do a straight-ahead comparison like that?"

"Yeah, which, you understand, usually means you have to break the glass. That's the only way to get a little piece to test it. And that pretty much ruins everything, so you can see what I mean by it being pretty impossible."

Usnavy nodded at the panels in Virgilio's hands. "Are they Armstrong? Can you tell that?"

Virgilio shook his head again. "They're better than Armstrong." He hobbled over to the apartment building and the silent domino game and came back, peeling bill after bill into Usnavy's hand, all Washingtons, with their wavy white hair (like Usnavy), more bills than Usnavy had ever dreamed of.

"Bring me the lamp," said Virgilio, shimmering now.

"The lamp?" a staggered Usnavy asked. His magnificent lamp? "I . . . I can't."

"Then bring me the one you already brought me . . . you haven't already sold it, have you? I'll fix it for you."

"Oh that one!" said Usnavy, rolling the bills into a ball like Frank might have and stuffing them in his pocket. "Yes, yes—I still have that one, yes."

"You got this glass from another one, right?" Virgilio asked cautiously.

Usnavy composed himself and ran his fingers through his white hair. "There are many others," he said, mentally inventorying all the lamps he had seen across town, especially the one he thought he'd seen at the Badagry woman's home, "many, many others."

In the weeks after the two red panels left Usnavy's hands, Nena's ID problem was finally solved, thanks to the temporary number and an accompanying U.S. bill discreetly placed in the palm of the clerk who, days before, could only shake his head. Jacinto's mother got her medicine and was soon full of vim and vigor again, washing clothes out in the courtyard. Jacinto himself was able to buy varnish and putty and began working to restore the treasures hidden in his room. He put studs on the pillars, secured them with rope and wire. In the meantime, Lidia and Rosita's sandwiches were now stuffed with single slices of canned Russian meat and sold at a profit on the streets of Old Havana.

Usnavy had gotten the small lamp fixed too, not by Virgilio but by one of his assistants, the older guy who always hung around in the rear of the studio, his back a slope, his hands strangely stained and deformed, but agile. His name was Santiago and he never made eye contact with Usnavy, only shuffled along, agreeing with a grunt to all of Virgilio's requests. Unlike Virgilio, Santiago did not sparkle, rather he seemed to sweep the light from the room. Usnavy would see him, a shadow, a manikin blowing bubbles, something unreal about him.

Once fixed, the small lamp was sold to a woman named Fay Reeve from Martinsville, Indiana, who claimed to know a real Tiffany when she saw one. "My aunt—she was just a young girl from Ireland then— she was with him when he died," she boasted of her connection to Louis Comfort Tiffany, never mentioning that by the time he passed, Tiffany was marginalized, a nineteenth-century anachronism, an embarrassment to American arts and crafts.

The profits from the sale to the lady from Indiana provided enough for two bikes—a new (used) Trek for Usnavy and a Flying Pigeon for Nena—a small Samsung color television, new shoes for him (the kind with multilevel soles) and Lidia and Nena, and a new (used) refrigerator. Usnavy was bewildered, dazzled, by what he found he could do for himself and his loved ones all of a sudden.

Now that there were dollars coming in, Lidia began to dream about driving again. "I can make more money that way than selling sandwiches," she said, having done the calculations. (Besides, she was a driver by training and disposition, that was her life.) "If we could buy a car, I could taxi," she continued, foraging in a box of Belgian chocolates for yet another piece, "and that's not just easier to disguise but it also brings in more money."

In immediate response, Usnavy went about his new business every day, riding up and down Old Havana on his new (used) Trek bike, pedaling easily in his new multilevel shoes, looking for the telltale sign of a light in the ruins. He looked for glints, for iridescent rainbow reflections, for the kind of color evoked by glass and bronze. He'd peer in windows shamelessly, cataloguing goods, jotting down anything he thought might be of interest later. Soon, very soon, he would have enough dollars for a car for Lidia. Very soon she'd be cruising happily through the city.

When not checking out the neighborhood—with its old colonial buildings, their walls leaning on the shoulders of those invisible giants Jacinto refused to believe in—Usnavy would spend hours sitting on the stoop, searching the skies for clouds and lightning. At the first raindrop, he would tear out of Tejadillo, his route all mapped out on his little notebook, zipping from one precarious building to another, looking for derrumbes. He could hear them before he saw them: a low groan buried deep in the pitter patter of the rain, a shriek when the wood surrendered, a sinister crack, and then *boo-o-oom*.

If at one point he had worried that his neighbors would view him critically if he ever ceased in his duty to the Revolution—which Usnavy interpreted, first and foremost, as an implacable honesty—he now realized that by engaging in *bisnes*, as the Cubans called it, he'd actually gained a respect he'd never enjoyed before. The neighborhood thugs who once greeted him out of habit or obligation now slapped his shoulder in camaraderie. Bizarrely, this made it easier to get them to clean up the tenement, to chip in to the CDR. When he and Lidia went out for an evening walk, he could feel the eyes of the others, not exactly envious but desirous of her place, of being suddenly able to relax a little, to put worries aside. If he was not entirely comfortable with his new status, he was at least fascinated by it.

These days, it seemed he was always prepared to dive into the mud and disaster of other people's lives (his new [used] bike secured with chains and locks he carried around his shoulder like a presidential sash), rescuing treasures to sell to Virgilio and his mute assistants—or, in the worst cases, to Yoandry, who took on not only the lamps and electrical fixtures that Virgilio rejected but anything from broken chairs to bricks to children's toys. However filthy he got in the process, he could wash it off. He could afford soap now, the good kind.

Soon after the sale of the small lamp, Yoandry had come rapping at Usnavy's door, sniffling and impudent, with his nicotine-stained fingers, eyeing Nena who, to Usnavy's dismay, returned his gaze.

"Get inside," Usnavy said to her sternly.

But an icy Nena ignored him. Instead she directed her eyes beyond him, to the continuing activity in the courtyard where every day, one or two groups would disappear through the arch of the entrance, never to be seen again. They'd stroll away, cocky and cool, dragging plastic bags and homemade rafts, each farewell pulling on Nena's own longing, he knew, like the tight, outstretched string of a crossbow.

"I said, get inside," Usnavy ordered again, then grabbed Nena's arm and dragged the sullen girl into their room.

Something had happened to her since the incident at the hotel, no matter that he'd gotten her the new bike and followed Lidia's advice to buy her a few other things too: perfumes, creams, new clothes. The girl he'd known, sweet and open, had disappeared into the countenance of this sour young woman. She dropped on the bed without saying a word, her arms across her chest, staring at the dullness of the lamp above her, lightless.

"What do you want?" Usnavy growled at the oily muscle boy outside.

"He's here, old man, that antiques dealer," Yoandry said through a smirk. He looked past Usnavy to the door, as if searching for Nena.

"What antiques dealer?" Usnavy asked as the door to his room popped open and a defiant Nena glared at him so hard and full of hate that he didn't have the wherewithal to stop her as she rolled her own bike through the labyrinth of activity in the courtyard and out of sight.

"You know what the man said," declared a snickering, mocking Yoandry: "'Silence is an argument carried on by other means.'"

Usnavy sighed. How was it possible that this boy could be so disrespectful?

Yoandry laughed. "Forget her for now, okay? I got more important stuff to talk to you about, old man."

"She's my daughter—you forget her, okay?"

"Whatever—listen to me: The antiques dealer, the one who's gonna buy your lamp and make us rich? He's here," the muscle boy said.

Usnavy grunted. "My lamp, huh?"

"Yeah, that one." Yoandry kicked open the unlocked door and pointed with his pimply chin at the magnificent one in the shadows, now hanging by both wire and rope in Usnavy's feeble attempt to keep it afloat in spite of the crumbling ceiling. (He had taken the opportunity while up there to check yet again for anything that resembled the Tiffany signature, but his lamp was still without an identifying mark, a bastard child.)

"Fire hazard, old man," Yoandry added, seriously. "That thing's gonna crash and shatter and then what are we gonna do, huh? You gotta do something about that. We should take it down, put it someplace."

Of course, the boy was right: But where? To bring it down from the ceiling in his room required moving the beds. Then where would they sleep? There was no way Usnavy would ever consider giving it to anybody else for safekeeping.

Usnavy waved him away. But Yoandry caught his wrist. "Don't do that," the boy warned, reversing roles with him from the day at the beach.

Usnavy yanked his wrist back. "Does Virgilio have a clue how you *really* are—how you are with everyone but him?"

"Virgilio and I are family, it trumps everything," Yoandry said, his cigarette dripping tobacco. "Now, family, you know about family, right, old man?"

He didn't believe for a moment this crude boy could be Virgilio's kin, but why argue? "What do you want?" he asked, exasperated, as he took some wire he'd brought from a derrumbe and coiled it around his arm. He'd cut a little to secure the lamp but he knew Yoandry would take the rest. That meant at least a dollar or, maybe, two.

"I want to talk about the lamp—*that* lamp," Yoandry said, "not the bullshit little one you brought Virgilio and me."

"Virgilio and you?" asked an incredulous Usnavy. "You said it was trash, remember?"

"Well, yeah," said Yoandry, the grin on his face just ugly now.

"Funny, you'd bring foreigners here but I bet you haven't told Virgilio about this other lamp, have you?"

"Not yet."

Usnavy scoffed. "Hell, Yoandry, you're not going to. You want to sell directly to the foreigner."

Yoandry laughed. "Hey, you're catching on—we skip the middleman. It's a bigger profit. Just you and me, we'll get a much better deal from the antiques dealer."

"But we'd get a better deal if Virgilio fixed the lamp. It has a few problems, you know."

Yoandry shook his slimy head. "Uh uh," he said. "We can sell this one right like this. Why go through all that trouble, huh?"

Usnavy knew why: The boy thought it was a Tiffany. He thought, even with the missing panels, that he could make such a good deal that he didn't need to risk getting Virgilio involved, having to share, or maybe getting left out altogether. Usnavy shook his head in disgust: The same lamp, the same artistry, he was sure, would be worth nothing to him if he knew it was probably made by some poor Cuban fool in Oriente and dragged to the city by an unsuspecting young woman and her misbegotten son. And that Cuban fool, he thought, was even worse off than Lam, Picabia, and Meucci. Nobody even knew his name to argue for him.

"Hey, I can bring that antiques dealer over right now if you want," Yoandry suggested, his palms touching and pointing in Usnavy's direction as if he were in church, even though there was nothing reverential about his gesture.

When the boy mentioned the antiques dealer, Usnavy imagined someone tall and rugged, like he supposed Mr. Tiffany had been, or perhaps like Burt (a quasi-American), only grander—in fact, like the Americans of his mind's eye, the ones he'd known in Caimanera and Guantánamo, sturdy and rowdy and even kind of amiable, if a little unintentionally condescending. (Mr. Tiffany surely would have fit right in among the officers at the base, Burt among the enlisted men.)

"C'mon, Usnavy, let's take down the damn lamp," Yoandry entreated. "I can spruce it up at the shop, I can store it. I can even put in some new glass on those empty slots. See, we don't need Virgilio for this. It'll make us rich."

"If it's my lamp, it's not going to make you rich now, is it? Not for sale," Usnavy said as he locked the door to his room behind him, guarding his treasure. A panel here and there he could do, he'd decided, because those could be replaced eventually—but to pack up and give away the whole thing? No way. If somebody ever got ahold of the lamp and had a chance to examine it, there would be no fooling anyone anymore. Then what would he have?

"Everything's for sale," countered Yoandry.

Usnavy stiffened. "Let's see if we understand each other, okay? The damn lamp is not for sale. It's my lamp, get it?"

"Yeah, but—"

Usnavy rolled right past him. "You're just a punk speculating about things you know nothing about. Not for sale—understand?"

"You're the one who doesn't understand," Yoandry said. "But you will."

Usnavy had been reading again, not just at the library, but at Virgilio's, where the silent gaffers recycled glass in huge barrels (most of it Coke-bottle green when it came out again) and the sparkly man spent hours hunched over a table, soldering little pieces of copper foil into panels for glorious lamps that would disappear in a day or two while countless others hung in the shop gathering dust.

Now that he'd become a regular, now that he'd gotten used to entering beyond the wall of heat at the studio door and knowing that he'd melt only a little with each visit, Usnavy had also begun to notice other things: that Virgilio only worked on lamps that were sold upon completion, that Santiago and the younger man, Manolín, often studied catalogues and old, yellowed magazines for hours to figure out designs.

Between turning pages in the old magazines and scratching the necks of Virgilio's plump cats, Usnavy would worry about the lamps that were there eternally, never meant for sale yet not quite decoration. They existed, Usnavy decided, as a distraction, so that if a visitor came only once or twice, he or she would think they would be sold like any other piece of merchandise. But they were too plain, too simple, too cheap. They were part of some larger scheme, this he knew.

Mr. Tiffany, he now determined, had been a man who aspired to art and a purity of spirit completely at odds with what made him famous. But those lamps of his—his signature pieces—were assembled in factories, churned out by the hundreds and thousands with little regard for art. Usnavy thought of Louis Comfort Tiffany not as a robust practitioner of capitalism but as its victim, a man simply too caught up in it to understand how it was killing him. His lamps existed solely to exploit electricity, the twentieth century's juice, to blunt its queer light, to make it mellow and safe.

The man died alone (regardless of what that woman from Indiana had said), Usnavy noted, his moment in the spotlight long gone, all those people who'd bought those lamps once thought of as treasures having moved on to the next thing, the lamps stowed away in basements and attics all over the eastern seaboard and Midwest of the United States. In a weird way, Usnavy felt for him, pitied him.

No longer keeping regular hours at the bodega, Usnavy had, in the meantime, become the focus of the CDR, which sent friends to search him out.

"Look, just come in the morning," Minerva said during a visit to the stoop at Tejadillo, where she found a fastidious Usnavy squinting at a hazy but sunny day.

He was listening to reports on his new (used) Walkman about the upcoming invasion of Haiti by U.S. troops and he was bewildered by the fact that they were actually going to reinstall a Marxist-leaning ex-priest as president, not topple him. It must be a trap, he thought, what else could it be?

A black cat peeked at him from a nearby rooftop, inscrutable.

"It could rain, don't you think?" Usnavy asked Minerva absent-mindedly, pointing at the sky. He listened for the murmur of a building in distress. He'd tried to check out Badagry's again—he'd convinced one of her sisters to let him take a look at her leaky ceiling, telling her he might be able to help put up posts like Jacinto. But he didn't get very close to the lamp because Badagry was home and stopped him cold at the door, saying they were moving soon, that the housing authorities had promised them a new place.

Usnavy's pulse had quickened. He knew that thing in there was treasure (whatever it was). She shouldn't have lied to him about having such a lamp, he thought; now that he was in business for himself, he would have bought it, he could have given her the money to fix their roof. Sometimes just the threat of rain could start things off . . . It was all a matter of paying attention. How long did she and her sisters have there? How long did he?

Minerva glanced up but couldn't read the signs in the sky that had Usnavy so enraptured. "Try to come by, at least in the morning," she repeated, back to her task. "You know, when they're all there. You can leave later. I'll cover for you."

"You have relatives in Pinar del Rio, right?" Usnavy asked.

She nodded, confused.

"You could call them and see if it's raining there, couldn't you? They have a phone, don't they?"

"You want me to call my family in Pinar del Rio to see if it's raining there? For the love of god, why don't you just watch the weather report?"

Usnavy shrugged. "They don't always get it right"—he pointed to the earphones wrapped around his head—"and I don't need to know about tomorrow. That's all they're going to tell me about, you know, tomorrow—always tomorrow. I need to know about now, about today, about a few hours from now," he insisted. "Whatever's in Pinar is headed here."

"What's so important about the weather report two hours from now?" Minerva asked with an arched eyebrow.

Usnavy got up from the stoop, dusted off his pants, and followed Santiago's example, shaking his head in disbelief, grunting, and walking away.

He sure wasn't going to give his secrets away to anybody.

Because, of course, now there were secrets. There had always been, certainly, but these secrets were grave and disorienting. They went beyond him and Lidia hiding what they were doing for dollars from Nena and the neighbors, beyond the white lies of ordinary life, yellow headlines and propaganda. They went beyond the peasant origins of his lamp, its shabby Third World pedigree.

They began to peek out of their hiding place when, needing to pull a few more dollars together so that Lidia could show a potential seller enough to have a shot at buying his car, Usnavy had extracted another glass panel from his magnificent lamp—this one not so loose but still easy to get at—and taken it over to Virgilio, who handled it with care but with less reverence now.

"So, are you ever gonna tell me where you get these, huh?" the artisan asked him.

Usnavy shrugged and shuffled, waiting for his money.

"I know they're coming from the same lamp, I can tell," Virgilio said. "And it must be quite extraordinary because these are not common pieces. They're a bit big, a bit unusual for a Tiffany. But they're definitely Favrile, definitely Tiffany."

A sparkly Virgilio handed the pane to Santiago, who took it away brusquely, practically tossing it at Manolín. Virgilio reached in his pocket as if to pay Usnavy.

"I'm thinking, Usnavy, that for all your revolutionary spirit, maybe your family was really part of the bourgeoisie, that you must have had a lot of money and influence once if they owned a lamp like that," he said, pulling his hands out of his pockets. All Usnavy could focus on was that those pockets were empty.

"I'm from Oriente," Usnavy said, unsettled. "Nobody had money in Oriente."

"Sure they did, all those sugar barons, all those Americans." Virgilio was now working on a small lamp, polishing the panels, as if he'd forgotten all about the payment due.

"Well, I'm not American. I'm descended from Jamaicans."

"You, Jamaican? Somebody's pulling your leg, my friend. What makes you think you're Jamaican?"

"My father was Jamaican."

"He was black?"

People made that connection frequently, and though most times Usnavy wanted only to say yes and confirm it, to claim a little bit of Africa in his blood, he found himself a little disappointed this time, surprised that Virgilio would respond in so common a fashion. "No, but you know, not all Jamaicans are black."

"Sure they are. The rest are called Englishmen. Nobody who's not black actually calls himself Jamaican. What's your last name anyway?"

"Martín Leyva."

Virgilio stopped cold.

Usnavy shifted his weight, now acutely uncomfortable. "Martín, it's English . . . Martín Leyva. Leyva's pretty common in Oriente, though not here."

"I'll bet!" said Virgilio, now grinning. "Tell me something, Usnavy: Was your mother a churchgoer?"

"No!"

"And your father?"

"I . . ." Usnavy stammered. He had no idea. "I never met my father."

Virgilio stared at him.

"What? . . . What?" a rattled Usnavy demanded.

"You, my friend, are a Jew," said Virgilio, "or, at the very least, the son of a Jewish woman—just like me."

A Jew . . . ? Hadn't Virgilio heard him? He was Jamaican—Jamaican, descendant of Africans and Englishmen, not Turks and Poles. Was Virgilio trying to get out of paying him? Usnavy turned on him. "You know, I've always thought you didn't look Jewish, that you look mulatto." He knew instantly his tone was accusatory and he stopped himself before this could go further: Anybody else might have said something about how Virgilio was trying to clean up his family tree, pretending to be Jewish rather than black. But what kind of insanity was that? Usnavy swallowed, the taste in his mouth vinegary and dry.

"Yeah, well, like I said, you don't look Jamaican—you look . . . American—actually, you look like an American Jew. I bet you were blond or red-haired as a kid, right?" Virgilio shot back at him, only he was smiling.

"This is ridiculous. I'm Jamaican," Usnavy repeated, annoyed.

"There are plenty of Jews in Jamaica."

Usnavy scoffed. "Yeah, right."

"*Yeah, right*—yes," insisted Virgilio. "The English didn't really bother them that much. You know, it's not so bad being a Jew. Maybe you're a Jamaican Jew."

"Look, this is a fascinating conversation, but are you going to pay me?"

"Yes, I'm going to pay you," Virgilio said, getting up from his workbench and wiping his hands. "But, whether you like it or not, your surname—your maternal surname—is Jewish. Not common Martínez/Ramírez/Rodríguez Jewish, but seriously, undeniably Jewish."

"This is crap," said a frustrated Usnavy.

Now it was Virgilio's turn to shrug. "Did you get the lamp from your mother?"

"The lamp . . . ?" Usnavy was miserable. How had the man switched from accusing him of being a Jew to the lamp?

"I think I know your lamp," Virgilio said.

"What the hell are you talking about? Look, just pay me, just pay me and let's end this conversation."

He wanted desperately to get out of there, to breathe real air, feel real light instead of the infernal heat and fairy dust falling off Virgilio.

But Virgilio held up his palm, signaling him to stop. "In good time, Usnavy Martín Leyva, in good time."

Usnavy shook his head. *Me, a Jew?* What did that mean anyway? Surely Virgilio was out of his mind. He wasn't taking on any new burdens, that was for sure. He was who he was, nothing more, nothing less. Usnavy was so agitated when he left Virgilio's that he walked most of the way home, for the longest time just holding the handlebars of his new (used) Trek and guiding it by his side.

During Usnavy's next visit, Virgilio explained that he and Santiago and most of the others in the building where he lived were descendants of old Jewish families—mostly immigrants from New York—who'd been living and working together since long before the Revolution. But the group did not simply repair lamps. What Virgilio and Santiago and the others really did for a living was create exquisite fake Tiffanies.

"My father did it, he taught me," Virgilio admitted with a laugh not unlike Yoandry's. "His father taught him. We've been doing it here in Cuba as long as there have been Tiffanies to counterfeit." He reached up and pulled a catalogue from a shelf, opening it to pages and pages of lamps, just like the ones all around him. "These are ours, all of them."

Usnavy stared at the color pages. "They're not Tiffanies?"

"They're Tiffanies, yes, but ours."

Usnavy ran his fingers through his white hair. "I see," he said, sitting down and dropping his hands flat on his lap.

"You don't," Virgilio replied, "but that's okay."

"Why's that okay?"

Virgilio shrugged. "It's hard to explain. For all the Tiffanies that are real, there are probably just as many that aren't. Those are ours—mine, my father's, my grandfather's. But the thing is, because my family worked for Tiffany, because my grandfather was who really got it right for Tiffany, you have to ask the question, don't you: Which Tiffanies are the real Tiffanies? Because if you're talking about the artistry that's known in the world as Tiffany, then that's ours. But if you're talking about the brand name, the industrial copyright, then that's his."

"What . . . what are you saying? That your family was the genius behind Tiffany lamps?"

"Hard to believe, huh?" Virgilio nodded nonchalantly. "Yeah, us—a bunch of Cuban Jews—we're the real Tiffany talent. Hell, we're the real Tiffany!"

Usnavy shook his head. "Forgive me, but I think you're delusional—that you're messing with me and think I'm too tired to tell." He smiled weakly as he got up.

"Sit down, Usnavy Martín Leyva, sit down," said Virgilio, his hand firmly on Usnavy's shoulder. "Remember when we were at the lamp store and we were talking about the Museum of the Revolution, and you said something about there being no stained glass there at all?"

Usnavy nodded wearily.

"Well, there's a reason for that, my friend. By the time Tiffany got that commission, Tiffany was doing everything—cabinets, tables. The man was all over the place. Anyway, originally, there was going to be a lamp at the palace, a huge and gaudy thing held by double suspension chains."

Oh god, thought Usnavy, his stomach churning.

"But then Tiffany and my grandfather had a falling out and the guild—you know, the guys my father had brought here with him—they refused to work for him," Virgilio continued. "Some people say the lamp that was supposed to go in the palace was made but never turned over to Tiffany. Others say it was never more than a drawing, and only a very rough one. With my grandfather's guys essentially on strike, Tiffany knew that if he wanted to use colored glass, he would have had to use inferior craftspeople. And if Tiffany was anything, he was a perfectionist. He knew the quality of work my grandfather did. He knew he couldn't use too much glass, if any, at the palace. Funny, isn't it? The palace is a Tiffany without the one thing for which Tiffany became famous: colored glass. Isn't that so typical of our little island?"

According to Virgilio, the grandfather felt he deserved to be paid for the idea of the lamps. And for his designs: He claimed the queen's lace was his, as well as the grapes and the peacock motifs. These were critical to the Tiffany catalogue. Tiffany was willing, if not happy, to pay, but not enough for Virgilio's grandfather, and the notion of credit was beyond him. So the artisan threatened to flood the market with phony lamps—and later knickknacks too—to punish him by forcing Tiffany prices down. It worked for a while, but then the market dried up and everybody was miserable, especially during the Depression.

Eventually, the price of Tiffanies—even the "fraudulent" ones—rose, as certain as the tides.

"One of his lamps sold at auction for more than a million dollars a few years back," Virgilio said. Then, looking around as if telling a terribly naughty secret, he whispered: "But the one that sold in 1985—it's a gorgeous piece—that was one of ours. And it went for more than half a million!"

"Was . . . was the lamp—the one for the presidential palace—was it signed?" Usnavy asked, his voice barely audible.

"Was . . . ? Was the lamp signed, is that what you asked? Aren't you listening? I just told you no one knows if it was ever even made!" Virgilio exclaimed. "I mean, if it was . . . *hufffffff!* Can you imagine?"

Usnavy's stomach dropped. He felt waves oscillating somewhere deep inside him. He wanted to surrender to the splendor and the ambiguity but Virgilio kept on talking, oblivious.

"Some people think it's out there—Yoandry, for one—but I don't think so," he said. "Somebody somewhere would have seen it by now, would have reported it back to us. I've seen a million Tiffany lamps here, or lamps that people think are Tiffanies, but are really god knows what. Still, nothing's even come close to what this thing was supposed to be. I mean, this is a small island, it's not like you could hide something like that."

"Yeah, but didn't you say no one knows if it was even made? Wouldn't that mean that no one knows what it would even look like? How would you identify it?"

"Yeah, I know, that's the problem precisely," said the sparkly man. "I've told Yoandry this but he insists. I guess it's a way of dreaming for him, for everybody who hears about it. A Cuban holy grail, I guess, something magical to look for. Something good finally, eh?"

A few days after Virgilio's revelations, with Usnavy still roiled by all of their possibilities, Frank showed up out of nowhere on Tejadillo. "Muchachón!" he shouted, hitting the door with the bottom of his hand.

"What the hell do you want?" asked a snarling Usnavy as he opened up.

He was in no mood for Frank and his twisted jokes, no mood at all for his not-so-funny and often cruel shenanigans. Lidia had left to price another Lada and all he really wanted to do was sit in the darkness and hold his head. A snotty Nena was off to school, whirling through the city on her bike. She disappeared for hours now, for what seemed like days, showing up late at night, immune to his and Lidia's grievances, and vanishing again at daybreak. Just the night before he'd caught her, he was certain, conspiring with the fleeing neighbors. She'd been whispering with some boys, passing them pieces of rope and wire from the stash Usnavy now kept to sell to Yoandry.

"What the hell are you thinking?" he'd asked, his fingers digging into the flesh of her arm as he yanked her away. He was so angry that she might actually want to leave—he didn't give a damn about the rope and wire—that he had to keep himself from hurling her against the wall or otherwise hurting her.

"Is it any different from what you're doing, huh? Is it?" she'd responded, her breath hot, her eyes moist and red.

As a result, Usnavy had woken up frazzled, his head throbbing and feverish. Looking out at Frank now, he scowled and spit.

"Whoa!" said Frank, throwing his hands up in the air as if in surrender. "What's up with you today?" Usnavy noticed his friend's heavy new watch, an anchor around his thin wrist: Money changing was apparently very good business these days.

"I'm asleep and you're bothering me, that's what," Usnavy said.

It may have been the first time in their lives that Usnavy had talked back to him, and Frank couldn't hide his surprise. But Usnavy's muscles were in knots.

"Hey, I just came to see how you were, if maybe somebody was sick. We haven't seen you at the game in a while and the folks at the bodega said you're on some kind of leave."

"That's because they won't fire me," Usnavy said, disgusted. "I haven't been there since I can't remember when, but, you know, I'm an exemplary worker so they don't have the guts to fire me. Who will explain it?"

Frank shifted his weight, tucked his shirt in. "Well, we haven't fired you either," he said. His Anthony Quinn face was soft around the edges of an incipient smile, rubbery and brown, like when they were boys together and he'd run home from his Quaker school, full of ideas he'd share with Usnavy and the others. They'd sit in awe of him, hearing him recount his knowledge, then they'd argue—Diosdado would start—and Frank would rub his then hairless chin.

"We're waiting for you, even Diosdado," said Frank, with his old voice, the slightly chagrined voice that he could never use to pronounce love and which always betrayed him. "And that's in spite of the fact that you are not an exemplary player and are, in fact, salao." Frank laughed and slapped Usnavy's shoulder.

But Usnavy was not amused. He was sick of being the butt of jokes, sick of being the extra man in the games. (If Obdulio returned tomorrow, he knew he'd lose his spot at the domino table, and that burned him.) Usnavy turned back into his room and returned with a huge wad of dollar bills.

"See this?" he said, holding the cash in Frank's stunned face, fanning the bills out with his fingers. The dollars were as crisp and green as lettuce. "Ever seen anything like this, huh? My friend, I am hardly the one who's salao."

And with that he slammed the door on a startled Frank and retired again to his cot, where he sprawled out on cool new sheets. He'd been listening to a Miami radio station earlier and he knew one thing for sure: It was going to rain later. In fact, it was going to pour.

Usnavy raged as he finally put his new multilevel shoe to the pedal of his new (used) Trek and headed to Tejadillo at the end of another day of scavenging. Forms blurred. The night smelled of sewage and salt, then a sudden flash of fragrance—something French perhaps, expensive. A tourist no doubt. Usnavy shook his head for clarity. His bike zigzagged through a maze of watermelon rinds thrown on the street. They looked like boats, overturned boats, a legion of boats.

In the beginning, there was water everywhere.

This is what he knew: His father had disappeared into the sea. He had vanished, over the rolling blue hills, into the horizon.

The damned circumstance.

On the Malecón, there was a party, a dance of some sort, spines curling. Nearby, a band was playing—a live band, a band in a house or apartment, a band with hand instruments—bongos, cajón, maracas, chekeré—*chak chak chak*—a rough rum voice. He thought he could see the singer's saliva misting the air.

Usnavy swerved, directed the snout of his new (used) bike away from the water, away from the stone columns, from the seawall. He spiraled around the groups of young people, laughter rising like steam, their mouths scarlet, feral.

The night is a perfumed insult on the beast's cheek; a sterilized night, a night without shame, without memory, without history, an Antillean night . . .

In the far corner of his eye, Usnavy spied a young woman—a girl, really, an adolescent: slender, long-limbed, with charcoal eyebrows and skin like wax. She carefully scaled the seawall: first up, leaning on the extended hand of a young man, just to the ledge, where they strolled like that, their fingertips barely touching, for what seemed a viscid and unreal time. She was carrying a satchel, something made of brown fabric or draft paper. The boy stretched his other hand ahead of him, into the air, the moist tropical air. And then they descended, both of them kneeling, then fading behind the seawall, throwing up a quick black flash of shadows cast by a beam from below.

"Say-hnor? Say-hnor?" A voice murmured into Usnavy's seashell ear: a voice with a fractured, staggering accent.

Where's the girl?

"Say-hnor? Say-hnor?" Somebody was pulling on his sleeve, with a laugh that gurgled weightlessly.

Usnavy thought his heart stopped for an instant. He tried to speak but his mouth opened to nothingness, only to his own torrid breath.

Nena? Nenita?

He rolled his head in dismay.

"Buddy, what you got? Fake cigars? Fake Lams? Fake lamps? Fake girls?"

Usnavy could sense the sea; he could feel the weight of the water pulling him down.

As soon as Usnavy heard the news the next day, he grabbed his bike and pedaled over to Montserrate, where the domino game was in full bloom. Neither Lidia nor Nena were to be found when he awoke; neither had been home when his eyes dropped their veil the night before and he had been too wiped out to resist. To his dismay, these days it wasn't unusual that either would be out late. But what struck him as peculiar was that he didn't hear either ever come in. Had he been that tired? Were they uncommonly quiet? Or was something else entirely going on?

As he neared the domino game, there were so many spectators that Usnavy couldn't even see the players. Besides a handful of the usual sapos—so many of these kept vanishing into the sea—all sorts of folks from the neighborhood were crowding the table, spilling out to the road, so that what few cars angled by had to slow down and slither around them. There were even women there too, women like Rosita who would normally scorn dominos, who might even resent the game because her current husband or lover found it more comforting than her company.

"Pssst, Usnavy!" Rosita motioned him toward her with a wave of the hand.

"I heard about Mayito," he said solemnly, scanning the crowd for Frank but not seeing him.

"Oh, that's old news," Rosita said with a dismissive wave.

"How can it be old news if I just heard it?" he asked, irritated, all the while thinking: Could it be possible? Had he drifted so far that no one would think to tell him that Mayito had left the country? That it wasn't on a boat like everybody else, like Obdulio, but with a real, honest-to-goodness visa procured by his long-departed wife?

"You're behind, that's all," Rosita said with a titter.

"So it's true?"

"Yes, yes—listen, Usnavy, don't feel bad." She touched his arm.

"Mayito didn't tell anybody, not even Frank. Actually, maybe least of all Frank. His wife got him that visa months ago; he was just sitting on it, trying to decide. And when he finally did, he only had a few days left on it before it expired. It wasn't a rash decision, he'd been thinking about it."

How could he not know any of this? How could he ever again say he and Mayito were friends? He wasn't so much bothered by the fact that he'd left—it was a surprise, sure, but in a way it didn't matter, everybody seemed to be leaving—but it gnawed at him that Mayito hadn't shared any of it with him.

Usnavy shook his head. This was, of course, the same damn reasoning Frank had used to humiliate Diosdado about his son that one day. How could he fall into this trap so quickly?

"So what is this—the world championship or something?" he asked Rosita, looking out at the game but still straddling his bike. He knew a bunch of the remaining sapos were already eyeing it jealously, and knew too that he wouldn't release it from between his legs no matter how long he hung out today. He tugged on the chains around his chest, not to show how secure they might be but as an implied threat, in case any of them decided they could take an old man.

Rosita leaned toward him and cupped her hands around her mouth: "It's Reynaldo—come back as a woman!"

Oh man, thought Usnavy: Too bad there were so few of the original sapos left in the crowd—they would certainly have good stories when they got home tonight! He craned his neck to look. "Where?"

For Usnavy, to imagine Reynaldo as a woman was to envision the boy he knew in a dress. Reynaldo's face would be the same, with barely a fuzz casting a shadow on his cheek; his new breasts would be a couple of dollops of flesh on his chest; his vanquished member nothing but a black hole.

Then he had a startling and disturbing thought: What if he couldn't recognize Reynaldo at all? What if Reina was actually a woman like any other woman? What if she could suddenly integrate and fade into any neighborhood, scars invisible to the human eye? He wondered what Mayito would have made of all this.

"What do you think, huh?" whispered Jacinto, who had sidled up next to Usnavy. "Do you think, if you were with her, that you could tell? I mean, *down there?*"

Usnavy flinched. But, in fact, he was thinking the same thing in his own way: What if nobody could ever really tell the truth about those around them? And what was the truth anyway? How many of the guys all around him might want to do like Reynaldo but didn't have a way, or the nerve, to follow through?

Usnavy surveyed the remaining sapos. He'd always thought he knew them, but now, between Mayito's flight and Reina's return, he wondered: Who are these guys? What are they capable of? Who can walk away and who will live forever wondering, doubting, yearning for what might have been?

The autistic boy sat in his chair, staring, unchanged and unchanging.

And what about him? What could the sapos tell about him that was perhaps indiscernible in the mirror's reflection? Had anyone figured out his secrets—the truth about his magnificent lamp? His mother? His father's mysterious disappearance? Did they know about his ambitions or fears? Could they tell how badly he missed Obdulio, how much he'd miss Mayito? Did they see that when it came to his only child, his heart was as cracked as most of the stuff under the rocks at a derrumbe?

Usnavy was dizzy with worry, his hands trembling on the handlebars.

"I think," said Jacinto abruptly, his voice still at a whisper, "that we're drawn to intimacy by all that mystifies us, you know? I mean, I'm looking at that girl, at Reina, and I want to be there, with her, inside her—Usnavy, she excites me—and she's a girl, sure, but part of it, for me, is what she was too, all the secrets on the path to—"

A startled Usnavy cut him off. "Hey—I'm not your psychiatrist, okay, Jacinto? Go to the doctor for that, you hear me?"

This was going too far, he thought, though he still hadn't been able to figure out who Reina was in that crowd. He started to turn the bike away, to inch out of the throng and go look for Nena, when he heard Frank.

"Oh, look who's here," he said with a facetiously flirtatious tone, but he wasn't talking about Reina, wherever she might be, but about Usnavy, with his bike between his legs and a wounded Jacinto at his side. "Look who has decided to grace us with his presence." Frank smirked, his rubbery Hollywood face back to its cruel tricks now that he had an audience. "Usnavy Martín Leyva, master of dollars!"

It was vintage Frank: mean, mean, mean. And, of course, now there was no Mayito to temper him. Usnavy shifted uncomfortably as the mob turned its envious eyes on him. He held tightly to the handlebars. Jacinto stepped back, suddenly appraising him.

"Usnavy?" asked a voice from inside the circle, an airy voice, like a flute playing a merry tune. It wasn't Nena. The sapos parted in surprise, almost in slow motion and with a strange deference. Usnavy's stomach lurched. There in the center of the throng was a lovely young woman in a spring print dress—a tasteful but common dress, nothing extravagant, nothing outrageous. Her shoulders sloped like Nena's, her hair was sandy and free flowing, cheeks flushed, and her mouth—it was the only thing that seemed out of place—was full, maybe too full.

Usnavy recognized Reynaldo immediately, or more precisely, recognized all the familiar gestures, the languor, the mind-boggling vulnerability. If in Reynaldo all those qualities had been frustrating and even alien, in Reina they were perfectly at home. She stood now with her hands on the shoulders of a vaguely attractive man—a foreigner—who'd been let into the domino game as a kind of indulgence.

"Usnavy . . . don't you remember me?" she asked, laughing a bit nervously.

This was unsettling for Usnavy. Reina's tone suggested a level of comfort between them he had never had. Why was she so friendly toward him all of a sudden? He pulled the bike up like an unruly colt, feeling the metal bar between his legs. Then he saw an anxious Diosdado looking up at him from the domino table, his eyes pleading.

"Of course I remember you," Usnavy said with a weak smile.

Reina beamed back, not just relieved but enchanted, her hands coming together in front of her surprisingly small breasts as if she were going to clap or pray (like Yoandry only days before). Diosdado fidgeted, unsure what to do, what to say; his eyes shiny like those of men who've been jailed or hospitalized too long. Usnavy's face flushed red, though he himself wasn't sure why.

Then the man whose shoulders Reina had been touching stood up, extending his hand toward Usnavy. "Hi, I'm Howard, Howard Reich—Reina's fiancé," he said in a muscular, masculine voice. He spoke nearly flawless Spanish. He was either young or young-looking, but not at odds with Reina. In fact, the glances he exchanged with her as he reached out to Usnavy revealed a generous lingua franca that rendered the bystanders quiet and amazed. "Good to meet you," Howard added as his hand clasped Usnavy's. It was a sure grip. (Later Usnavy would wonder why this surprised him.)

Howard was blondish, much like the Americans at Guantánamo

from Usnavy's childhood, with hay-yellow streaks floating on top of darker, richer, healthy hair. He dressed well, but casually, with the ease that comes with real wealth: Usnavy realized it was all in the manners and accessories—the simple but exquisite wristwatch, the thin but elegant belt, the fact that his linen shorts were pressed.

If your son is going to become a woman and bring home a man, thought Usnavy, *then this one is not so bad.* In an unguarded moment, he could admit Howard pleased him enough for Nena, at least initially, and especially when he thought back to the creepy moment with Yoandry at the door to his room. All in all, Diosdado might be lucky after all.

Howard sat back down and refocused on his dominos.

"What . . . ?" asked Frank, obviously not happy that Usnavy had managed the introduction without stumbling and surprised that both Howard and Reina seemed to be especially open to him. "*Rrrrrreina*"— Frank pronounced her name with sarcasm, dragging the R—"now you like him better than me?"

Frank's move was nasty not because Usnavy had ever been especially close to Reynaldo—whom he never understood, whom he wished would just stop being such a source of anguish to his father (this wish never translated into anything concrete, though: Usnavy never asked the forces of the universe to make Reynaldo different one way or the other, just to stop being a problem, that's all)—but because, in fact, it was Frank who had often been provocative toward the boy, calling him a faggot to his face when his father wasn't around, making derisive comments about him left and right, and, at least once, threatening him with a beating if he ever stood behind him again.

What Frank was doing now was an unthinkable breach of etiquette. It was fine that Frank did what he did behind Diosdado's back; it was even acceptable that he should poke at Diosdado with all sorts of sadistic innuendos and drive him crazy. But it was never okay to embarrass anyone in public like this: Offspring were a joy or a shame, but still the crown of their elders, nature's unpredictable creatures.

The remaining sapos were visibly stunned by Frank too, as if caught in a freeze-frame. Diosdado seemed to disappear behind his dominos, his skin a paler shade by the minute, hands slick from perspiration. Usnavy thought Diosdado might actually cry. What could that poor man do here in his own defense?

"I always liked almost anybody better than you, Frank," Reina said. She flashed him a hard smile; her eyes cold black bullets. Then she placed her hand on Howard, who did not betray any emotion. Diosdado seemed both startled and oddly pleased.

"Even good ol' cursed Usnavy?—cause he's salao, you know," Frank snickered. He shoved a cigar in his mouth and lit it dramatically, but Usnavy could tell he'd been caught off guard by the girl. Without Mayito around, it was as if Frank had no center, no compass.

"Enough," said a steady Howard in his textbook Spanish, not bothering to even look up at Frank. To Usnavy, the foreign fellow's face was so still, so emotionless, it seemed as though he wasn't really speaking, but that he was throwing his voice instead: It was as if his words appeared in the air, unconnected to anything, like biblical pronouncements perhaps.

"Enough?" Frank asked incredulously. He'd been leaning back in his chair and this caused him to drop down to the ground. "Enough what, *mees-ter*?"

Usnavy looked around desperately.

"I thought we were playing," said Howard, expressionless still, his eyes on the black and yellow pieces in his hand. "I thought you would teach me this game Cuban-style, which I've heard so much about."

Then, out of nowhere, the sapo sitting in for Mayito—Oscar Luis, the cab driver—dropped a domino into the middle of the table: a double two. The others gasped. It was a lousy opening but that was not what really jolted them: Their representative, the stand-in for Frank's most loyal of lieutenants, was not playing along with Frank. Oscar Luis looked Frank right in the eye, undeterred, daring him. The story was getting better.

"What the fuck is that?" Frank protested, flustered.

Sensing his helplessness, the sapos laughed, loud and hearty.

"Just play, Frank," Oscar Luis said firmly.

Then—with Frank's shaky fingers hovering above his pieces as they stared each other down—a distracted Jacinto inadvertently stepped into the act. "She's beautiful, isn't she?" he said to no one in particular. He gazed at Reina: It was pure admiration, nothing lascivious or ugly in it.

Usnavy lifted a finger to his lips, signaling quiet. Was this man nuts?

Then one of the sapos—a mechanic named Ernesto—snapped in the war veteran's direction: "It's all plastic, man, so don't go getting too excited."

"What? What now?" Frank demanded from the table. His hand was a fist like Yoandry's, but not as big, not as hammy.

The malevolent Ernesto grinned, showing holes in his teeth. "Jacinto here thinks she's beautiful, man," he said, pointing at Reina with a lewd finger.

The other sapos rustled, mortified. Diosdado seemed to be on the verge of a nervous breakdown. His lips were open in an O, a ring of saliva dried white and chalky around them. There was a huge arch of sweat under his arms now, and perspiration was dripping from his brow, clouding his glasses.

But none of this mattered: Reina stood with her neck white and swanlike in the midday sun. Here was a woman, Usnavy could see, who would be deemed perfect by the crowd under any other circumstance. Here was a woman who could wait forever if necessary while her man took care of business in a bar or vestibule somewhere; she would not sigh in exasperation, she would not complicate matters by letting strangers get too close, she would not pretend to busy herself with banalities such as filing her nails. Instead, she would pull a paperback from her bag, or maybe do a little window shopping without straying too far (and possibly even pick up a little something for her beau—a sack of roasted peanuts, a flower for him that she would later wear in her hair); most likely she would lean against the wall, or cross her legs discreetly while on a couch or park bench, and watch the world around her—the mothers and their litters of children, the tired women and men crawling home from work, or creeping out for the evening, still adjusting their bra straps or belts.

Diosdado just seemed to gape at her: *Reynaldo? Is that really you?*

"She is beautiful," Jacinto asserted, tipping an imaginary hat at her like his father back in the sepia portrait in his room. He gave Howard a congratulatory nod.

"What is the matter with you people?" a furious Frank exclaimed. All of a sudden, he slammed his pieces flat on the table. The sapos peeled back.

A resigned Oscar Luis folded each one of his dominos facedown, like miniature coffins.

"Have you all lost your mind?" Frank demanded, getting up now, his simian arms held out from his body.

Poor Frank, Usnavy thought with a sudden realization: Nobody waits for him, there's nobody to pretend not to see his faults, nobody to offer love's great gift of forgiveness.

Then Howard stood up, lifted his hand in Reina's direction, and pulled her toward him protectively. A trembling Diosdado rose too, his pieces having been turned down already, and in some sort of awkward and unspoken covenant with Howard, muttered apologies to those around and stepped away from the game. Both his shirt and pants were soaked, clinging to him like a giant jellyfish.

"Where do you think you're going, huh?" Frank rasped, jumping up and down in place, but he was getting smaller and smaller as he squirmed and thrust his chest at the visitors. "Come back here!"

That's when a jaunty Jacinto took a seat at the table and began to stir the domino soup as if nothing unusual at all was taking place. Frank looked at him, confused. Who the hell did this guy think he was?

"You in, Usnavy?" Jacinto asked. Oscar Luis, sitting next to him, laughed aloud, enthusiastically. Even the autistic boy's lips seemed to quiver into a tentative smile.

Usnavy didn't hesitate: He jumped from the bike, sat down, and fished out his pieces.

This was a great story. Lidia, and even Nena—wherever she was, whatever she was doing—would love it.

VI.

That night, the sky was smoky and blue. It promised rain, it promised thunder. The stars were bright smudges. A just-washed Usnavy wandered around the courtyard, restless, his shirttail flapping behind him. He was obsessed with Nena's whereabouts—he hadn't actually laid eyes on her in a day or so and he could hardly keep still from worry. He kept glancing over his shoulder, his hand trembling. He tried to calm down by pacing, tried to focus on something else: He counted his steps, he cracked his fingers.

Okay then, he thought: Badagry—after so many years as an officer of the CDR, after so many marches and speeches, didn't he know anybody at the housing authorities to whom he could take their plight? The women could move—he had no problem with that!—he'd even help. But first—yes, first, he wanted . . . How could he even phrase what he wanted?

Where the hell is Nena? Where? At first he'd thought Lidia would know but she was as lost as he, though less worried, more distracted with their *bisnes*. But Lidia hadn't been to Cojímar, she hadn't been down to the Malecón, she hadn't seen what he had seen, she was not being haunted by ghosts. How could he explain all those bodies, like white crabs rushing toward the surrounding waters?

At Tejadillo, his neighbors sat at their doors. He could feel them

watching him stride from one end of the crowded, obnoxious courtyard to the other, sidestepping the packing and raft-making which had
now become central to the tenement. The hammering was relentless,
the pounding arrhythmic and brutal. Some of the neighbors sucked on
cigarettes, others chatted but in whispers now, everyone saving their
energy for the longer, more treacherous voyage ahead. Smoke and vapor twirled up into the skies, blue and white.

Against a wall, a teenager was juggling a bag of marbles; another
continuously shuffling a deck of cards. A skeletal cat tangled himself in
an elderly woman's bare legs, then leapt up to her lap and nuzzled hard,
ramming his head under her chin. A little boy with dirty buttocks and
wearing nothing but an undershirt stacked dominos, not to knock them
down with a bright and wonderful swirl, but like building blocks. These
were wooden dominos, once extravagant but now worn from use, a
hand-me-down. Usnavy watched as the kid built a second story, then a
third, before the whole wobbly structure collapsed. No one even looked
up from their carpentry and boat-making.

"Usnavy?"

He turned around fast, only to catch Howard and a complicit Yoandry standing right behind him. Cumulus clouds of nicotine obscured
Yoandry's face.

"Hello."

"Is there someplace we can talk?" asked Howard, calm as the waters on
a northern lake, never knowing hurricanes or typhoons. He looked around,
above, through Usnavy's neighbors, never quite fixing them in his sights.

Next to him, Yoandry bit at the inside of his cheeks, his shoulders
hunched. He was actually built bigger, better, stronger, but he seemed di-
minished somehow, as if his form was all air, his bones nothing but string.

"We can talk here," Usnavy said, sweeping the courtyard with his hand. For a second everyone stared, unabashed; oddly, he felt he needed the comfort of their company. The cat dropped from the woman's lap to the ground, bared its teeth, and hissed at nothing in particular.

"We can talk in your room, that would be better," Howard replied coolly.

"No, my family's in there, my daughter's sleeping," he lied. (Then, for a second he thought, maybe she is in fact there—he considered how they'd laugh later, him so consumed by worry when all along she was napping . . .)

Yoandry widened his eyes, sending him signals he refused to acknowledge.

For Usnavy, it was all instinct. Nena was a mystery. Lidia was out, busy with her new obsession, checking out another possible car purchase. None of the others had worked out. And this one would be complicated because the car was brand new: Usnavy and Lidia would have to divorce (they would explain it to Nena—she was old enough, she would understand), Lidia would have to marry the Russian diplomat who as a foreigner had the right to buy a new car, and shortly thereafter, divorce the diplomat, taking with her in the settlement the right to the car. Then and only then would she and Usnavy be able to get their hands on what they'd hope would be an air-conditioned Mitsubishi. If they could pull it off, life seemed to be guaranteed. It would cost him a good chunk of the lamp and a lot of traipsing up and down Old Havana, but once Lidia started driving, Usnavy knew they'd make the money back and he could replace the missing pieces on the lamp, good as new—maybe even better than new.

Nena, he thought, would be taken care of.

It was hot in the courtyard.

"Usnavy, do you speak English?" Howard asked.

"No." Nena was studying English at school; if she were here, maybe she could help . . .

"Do you speak any language at all except Spanish?"

"No."

Howard sighed. "Very well. My friend here, Yoandry, tells me you have a lamp I might be interested in. I understand my business partner, Burt, got a quick look at it as well."

This, he figured, is why Reina had been so friendly; it had had nothing to do with him, with any kindness he'd ever extended. It was the lamp; it was *bisnes*; it was money.

"I have access to lots of lamps. What are you looking for?"

"I am looking for a lamp that was made for the Presidential Palace but was never installed," Howard said. He could have been talking about the weather.

Usnavy ran his hand through his white hair. "People keep talking about that lamp."

Like a clumsy spy, the skeletal cat tiptoed toward them, craned his neck.

"It's your lamp," whispered an impetuous Yoandry. It was clear he did not want the neighbors to hear. He mouthed: "The one in your room." Then he kicked the cat, which shrieked and disappeared into the chaos around them.

Howard gave the boy a stern look.

Usnavy closed his eyes for an instant. Tonight, outside the tenement, he prayed, the city would slope down to the sea, bright and rugged, meeting the water with a kiss. He imagined not traders or tourists, but natives splashing about, the sea full of marlin and flying fish, tiny, tiny silver things that looked like sparks underwater. The eyes of his neighbors were pelicans, herons, and cranes.

"The lamp I have is not that lamp," Usnavy finally explained. He had to buy some time here, telling them without showing. The lamp was riddled with missing panes, holes. He couldn't imagine letting go of it. "It was my mother's lamp, it was never a Presidential Palace lamp. How would my mother, who was nothing but a simple woman, ever get her hands on a presidential lamp, huh?" He was going with the truth that he knew, not as a strategy per se, but because he couldn't think of anything else to say. The neighbors perked up, twitched as they worked.

Howard shrugged. "You never know. If you show it to me, I could tell you. It could be worth a lot of money if it's the one I'm looking for."

But as Usnavy's feet (in those wonderful new shoes) began to squish in the water perennially underneath his soles, he felt a drop on his head. It was more like syrup or honey. He tilted his chin up, receiving another, then another. In the distance, a whistle and grunt then a groan came from deep inside somewhere.

Wordlessly, Usnavy turned away from Howard and the muscle boy, away from the turbulence in the courtyard, and toward the rain and the hazy sky.

At the derrumbe, just blocks from his own home, Usnavy dug through the freshly fallen bricks and rocks like a dog after a bone. After the rage of rain and wind had become nothing but a whisper, he dropped to his knees and used his bare hands, scratching at the cement to get underneath the wreckage, scraping at the dirt, the wet plaster, the ripped fabric of old laundry, the crumpling cardboard, the corroded tin, the rotten wood, the rusted steel pins, the oxidized nails. He did not think of Badagry, of where she was, of her sisters and whether they were alive.

He dug and dug and dug: Somewhere underneath there was that

damn lamp—he had taken quiet measure of its dome, had registered the lead molding so that he could almost taste the metal on the back of his own tongue, had understood immediately from the way Howard and Virgilio talked about the presidential lamp that this was as close as he could hope to get to the treasures of Alexandria and the pyramids.

When it began to pour, Usnavy ran—ran and ran (he ran easily now)—ran right past Howard and Yoandry and the kids splashing about outside, because he knew the house down the street would quake, knew it could lose a limb or two with each new drizzle, knew that, finally, its joints would surrender, its foundation would fold, its muscles would hiss and sputter and everything would come down to crush the invisible sleeping giant who had been miraculously holding up the paper walls, this weird miracle of Cuban architecture. He knew too that this was it; this was the moment he'd been waiting for.

Now Usnavy dug, his fingers feeling through the viscera of the flattened, imperceptible titan: its sticky bodily fluids, its softened tendons, its jagged bone fragments. When Usnavy pricked his palm and pulled it up to see the cut—a stream of blood flowing smoothly from the wound interrupting the curve of his lifeline—he bared his yellow teeth and smiled. There was no other glass in that house, its windows had been open to the elements, there were no mirrors, barely any plates, zero knickknacks, no toiletries—there was no doubt in his mind: The bit of blood now wiped on his pants was the sure sign he'd struck gold. Whatever pane was fractured or lost could be replaced, like on his own lamp—glass was ageless, untraceable, Virgilio had assured him; no one would ever know.

Usnavy reached under the rocks, grunting and wailing, thrashing and pulling, finally wrapping his fist on something long and plump—not the lamp, no, but some other treasure, something for Yoandry perhaps, a little something before finally reaching the lamp. He sucked in air and yanked as hard as he could on what might have been wire or cable, his lungs almost exploding, his spine extending, arching until he fell backwards, tumbling down the garbage heap, the tower of terrible treasures.

When Usnavy finally stopped rolling and falling, his shirttail twisted and his waist poked by something sharp, he thrust himself up on an elbow, noticing he was lying in a puddle that smelled of both petroleum and urine, and took a good look at what he had in his grip.

It was roots and earth, black and fertile and wet. But his hand was wounded, the bone jagged, his fingers stabbed by shards of colored glass and bloated like petals on a flower.

When Usnavy limped home that night, Tejadillo was desolate. It was starting to rain again. The drops felt like pinpricks on his skin, sharp and cold. There were no lights in his courtyard, no human sound or movement. It was a lunar landscape, austere, overwhelming. The water was rattling where the funnel of flies that had been the bathroom once stood, now just a pile of glistening rubble. He touched his chest where his heart might be, felt its slight beating. He looked ahead and saw through the darkness the barrel of water outside his door sprinkled with rocks. The door itself was outlined by light.

Like a somnambulist, Usnavy started to walk through what had once been the courtyard of his home, holding his bleeding right hand ahead of him the whole time, but he tripped on something and tumbled. He exhaled, his breath warm and acrid. His body felt wrenched, contorted against the bitter ruins. Still, he lay there for a while, shivering, unable to move, his fingers numb. He was chilled and soaked and alone. A cat with something dark and squirmy in its mouth brushed by, going about its own business, barely glancing at him. At one point, he realized the

wooden planks beneath him were the remnants of a raft, left unfinished
by his neighbors. He rubbed his sun-blotched face against the grain,
pressed his nose to it. Then, with a heave, Usnavy hauled himself up
until he pushed past the glowing door of his room. He closed his eyes for
an instant, held his breath. Whole walls had crumbled on one side yet
the ceiling, though buckled, swooned in place. The light that gave the
threshold its aura was coming from the new (used) refrigerator, tilted
now, its door unhinged, its tiny bulb a beacon. The floor was a slippery
swamp but the rest was more or less there: the beds filled with debris;
the new TV set crushed by a piece of concrete. Water ran everywhere,
between rocks, chunks of walls, a neighbor's toy truck.

But—thank god!—neither Nena nor Lidia was there: They were
surely elsewhere, safe. Usnavy sighed, lips aquiver, his stomach turning,
all the bile that he'd been holding inside streaming out his mouth and
nose. He wiped his face with his good hand, ran his fingers through his
stringy hair, now brown and brackish. On the floor, loose pages from
Martí swam in the muddy currents. An inflated anonymous paperback
caught them between its own pages, then bumped up against the back
cover of something else.

Finally, Usnavy leaned against the wall, not wanting to look up:
The lamp was hanging by a strand from the improbable hunk of ceiling,
its remaining glass shattered, the black holes of the missing panels like
rotten teeth. Its shadow draped the room like the suspended, battered
cadaver of a giant jungle cat.

Usnavy couldn't think. He fumbled his way to his cot and, with his
working left hand, picked the sheet up by the corner, shaking the dirt
and rocks from it. He lay down and pulled the sheet over his shoulder,
tugging his injured arm inside, close to his chest. It was sticky with
blood, warm still.

Usnavy stared at the shadows around him. Was it just his room? The end of the earth? The backside of his own eyelids? He wished with all of his might to look out over an island with no water, surrounded by nothing but air. He shut his eyes, tight, seeing the island rise above the world, as if after some sort of apocalypse.

Usnavy turned on his side and felt the bits of rock on the bed poke and pinch him. He tried to picture himself walking along the contours of the shore, feeling the breeze, soaking in the clear and unfettered light from all around.

Usnavy was asleep when Lidia found him the next morning. The rain was still rushing down, leaking through various holes in the ceiling and rioting. Lidia saw that he was breathing and started to cry.

Jacinto, his hair covered with dust, found her like that, sitting at Usnavy's side. (If Usnavy had been awake, he would have imagined Jacinto like the slaves who brought rice to the New World, grains hidden in his hair.)

"How is he?" Jacinto asked, shaking his head clean.

"Sleeping," Lidia said. "I don't want to wake him, not yet."

"My mother made some coffee," Jacinto offered. Lidia looked up at him, puzzled. "She's in my room. We're okay—I had put up supports. I thought this might happen. Let me tell her you're here."

Lidia nodded and Jacinto stepped out for a moment. When he returned, he sat down next to her and placed his arm around her shoulder.

"Hey . . . we can rebuild," he said, his voice soft but buoyant. "We always rebuild, don't we? And didn't I hear you're about to get a car— Lidia, you'll be up and fine in no time."

"Screw the car," she said and started to cry again.

Just then Jacinto's mother came in with a little tray carrying steaming demitasses. The coffee rippled in the cups—she was unsteady. Jacinto handed one to Lidia, using his fingertips to carry it. Then Usnavy stirred on the bed, his teeth chattering.

"Don't sit up," Lidia cautioned, putting her cup back on the tray and guiding Usnavy's to his lips. Jacinto reached around and held the old man's head up, so that his lips could feel the heat from the cup, his tongue the sweet sting of the burning liquid.

After he was finished, Usnavy sat up and looked around him, surveying the destruction. His eyes settled on the lamp above them.

"It's . . . it's still here," he said, his voice cracking.

Lidia and Jacinto glanced at each other with concern.

"I'm glad it's still here," Usnavy whispered, then choked a little and coughed. The fingers of his left hand played almost imperceptibly on the bed and rolled a piece of gravel, a smooth little pebble, around on the sopping sheet. "Nena . . . ?" he muttered, a faint ripple on faraway waters.

Lidia shook her head ever so slightly. Her eyes were moist and shimmered.

Usnavy squeezed the pebble in his good hand, scratched the dirt from it, stroked it discreetly like a talisman.

"Ay . . ." Usnavy said, his voice hoarse, his face smeared with dirt. "It's just . . . just like . . . just like . . ."

"Please don't talk," said Lidia.

Jacinto stood and leaned against what was left of the wall.

"It's like with Africa," Usnavy said. "Africa and its curse . . ." He stared off at the lamp. It was gray now that daylight was creeping into the room. It was a mess: a splintered tibia, a mangled rib cage.

"I can probably fix that." Jacinto followed Usnavy's gaze to the lamp. "You wouldn't believe how good I've gotten at fixing things."

Usnavy realized Jacinto really believed he could.

"I can fix it, I swear to you," insisted Jacinto. "Hey, we're a nation of giants. Aren't you the one who's always saying that? You'll see, it'll be fine."

"But you don't believe in giants, Jacinto, you put up those posts," Usnavy mumbled. With his right hand still hidden under the sheet and his left holding the pebble, he shifted and sat up a bit more. A few bits of gravel rolled off him to the ground. "And look, you were right . . ."

Jacinto was flustered, obviously unsure about how to deal with what he was hearing. "You just get better, Usnavy, and we'll fix it together. Now, let's get you to a hospital, okay?"

Usnavy rolled the sheet around his right wrist and hand. The blood underneath was coagulated and black but oozed a bit.

"Let me see that," Lidia said the instant she got a glimpse of the red blotch.

Usnavy shook his head. "At the hospital."

As they crossed the courtyard and the funnel of flies, a party of tourists exploring the derrumbe met them midway. Usnavy thought he recognized the guide from the day Diosdado had refused to have his picture taken.

"Look at that," said one of the tourists—suddenly, Usnavy understood her English perfectly. He followed her eyes to something in the remains: It was a nugget of rainbow—ruby, emerald, imperial gold—there amidst the broken walls, rusted steel spokes, shredded paperback books, and the inevitable orange slush from the tenement's fluids.

"A light in the ruins!" barked a man with a camera.

Usnavy cringed.

The tourist snapped a photo, delighted with his find, looking right through Usnavy as he trudged by, held between Lidia and Jacinto.

* * *

At the hospital, an emergency room crew unveiled the injury—Lidia gasped and immediately opened a new cascade of tears when she saw it. The wound was black, almost green, its odor salty and pungent, like rotting mollusks.

The surgery to save Usnavy's hand was executed under a portrait of Che with the legend *Until victory, always* and a long frosty tube of fluorescence, without anesthesia because there simply wasn't any. Instead, the doctors had Lidia, Jacinto, and a couple of volunteers hold Usnavy down while they treated him. Their fingers dug into his skin, leaving strings of blue-green bruises like ancient beads. All the while, his teeth bore into a piece of black rubber—maybe the remnants of a fan belt from a still vibrant Ford or Buick.

After the operation, a drained Usnavy, his mouth open and maroonish, was put to bed as Lidia and Jacinto took turns watching over him. Jacinto's mother dropped by, now in the full glow of health. Minerva from the bodega read him the headlines from *Granma*. Even Frank and Diosdado, on good behavior for their friend's sake, showed up with Oscar Luis, the cab driver, retelling favorite stories from the domino game on Montserrate.

They knew about Nena but talked only obliquely about her absence. And they had some news too: The autistic boy, it turned out, had also left the island on a raft, the winds pushing him every which way so that he landed in Haiti, just as the U.S. marines were setting foot on Boukman's native soil.

"How salao is that, huh?" asked Frank in his slightly chagrined voice.

As his friends watched over him, Usnavy rested under a thin sheet, the future of his fingers uncertain, his pulpy palm a nest of scars like Virgilio's fingertips. He tossed and turned, his eyelids fluttered.

"I need some rest," he said, barely audible and to no one in particular. His lips were dry and sticky, his tongue stabbing at them with its parched tip. "We all need some rest." He could see himself greeting those who stayed and those who left, Nena too.

Abruptly, Usnavy turned, rearranged his body—numb and heavy—to face the wall on the other side of the bed.

I want to die old and contented, he dreamt, *in the soft dapple of a primal Antillean night.*

Also available from Akashic Books

HAVANA NOIR
edited by Achy Obejas
360 pages, trade paperback original, $15.95

Brand new stories by: Leonardo Padura, Pablo Medina, Achy Obejas, Carolina García-Aguilera, Ena Lucía Portela, Miguel Mejides, Arnaldo Correa, Alex Abella, Moisés Asís, Lea Aschkenas, and others.

"A remarkable collection . . . Throughout these 18 stories, current and former residents of Havana—some well-known, some previously undiscovered—deliver gritty tales of depravation, depravity, heroic perseverance, revolution, and longing in a city mythical and widely misunderstood." —*Miami Herald*

CHICAGO NOIR
edited by Neal Pollack
270 pages, trade paperback original, $14.95

Brand new stories by: Achy Obejas, Bayo Ojikutu, Alexai Galaviz-Budziszewski, Adam Langer, Joe Meno, Peter Orner, Claire Zulkey, Daniel Buckman, and others.

"Any collection of stories that features one about a Cuban drag queen named Destiny that begins with her smoking a 'short, slim and brown Romeo y Julieta' cigar and drinking a 'wee cup' of espresso poured from an 'hourglass-shaped coffee maker' is off to a good start. 'Destiny Returns' by Achy Obejas is just one of the 18 new stories in this latest geographic outing from Akashic." —*Chicago Tribune*

HAVANA LUNAR
a novel by Robert Arellano
200 pages, trade paperback original, $14.95

"A sad, surreal, beautiful tour of the hell that was Cuba in the immediate aftermath of the collapse of the Soviet Union. The writing is hypnotic, the storytelling superb. *Havana Lunar* is perfect."
—Tim McLoughlin, author of *Heart of the Old Country*

"Written with passion and vision and with a clear, unflinching eye, *Havana Lunar* breaks new ground . . . I am certain that [it] will find a wide and enthusiastic readership." —Pablo Medina, author of *The Cigar Roller*

ADIOS MUCHACHOS
a novel by Daniel Chavarría
246 pages, trade paperback original, $13.95
*Winner of a 2001 Edgar Award

"A zesty Cuban paella of a novel that's impossible to put down . . . a great read."
—*Library Journal*

"A steamy, sexy, kinky, pulpy mix of comedy, mystery, and murder." —*Booklist*

"Daniel Chavarría has long been recognized as one of Latin America's finest writers."
—Edgar Award–winning author William Heffernan

TANGO FOR A TORTURER
a novel by Daniel Chavarría
390 pages, trade paperback original, $15.95

"A one-time Argentine revolutionary exacts an inventive revenge on the ex-military man who once did him a horrible wrong in this superior crime novel . . . The author, who lives in Havana, brings to his novel a superlative narrative sense, keen feel for human behavior in desperate situations and a deep understanding of the nature of dictatorships. Chavarría is as adept at comedy as he is at tragedy."
—*Publishers Weekly* (starred review)

THE AGE OF DREAMING
a novel by Nina Revoyr
320 pages, trade paperback original, $15.95

"*The Age of Dreaming* elegantly entwines an ersatz version of film star Sessue Hayakawa's life with the unsolved murder of 1920s film director William Desmond Taylor. The result hums with the excitement of Hollywood's pioneer era . . . Reminiscent of Paul Auster's *The Book of Illusions* . . . [with] a surprising, genuinely moving conclusion." —*San Francisco Chronicle*

Ross Furman

ACHY OBEJAS is the author of various books, including the award-winning novel *Days of Awe* and the best-selling poetry chapbook *This Is What Happened in Our Other Life*. She is the editor of Akashic's critically acclaimed crime-fiction anthology *Havana Noir*, and the translator (into Spanish) for Junot Díaz's Pulitzer Prize–winning novel *The Brief Wondrous Life of Oscar Wao*. Currently, she is the Sor Juana Writer in Residence at DePaul University in Chicago. She was born in Havana and continues to spend extended time there.